A M

Christie's excitement at her new job was dashed when Lyle Venniker turned up as her boss. But why did he hate her so much? Hadn't she given him what he wanted—his freedom?

Books you will enjoy
by YVONNE WHITTAL

CAPE OF MISFORTUNE

Bored with her life as a teacher in Durban, Emma Gilbert leapt at the chance of a year in Mauritius as governess to little Dominic; but the mysterious death of the child's mother and the disturbing nature of his father, gave her the feeling of being prey to a serpent in this earthly paradise...

THE DEVIL'S PAWN

The marriage between the arrogant Vince Steiner and Cara Lloyd was not in name only—despite the fact that it was just a twelve-month contract between them. It was one more way to humiliate Cara's father. But there was nothing in the contract about love—and that could prove humiliating for Cara...

WILD JASMINE

Returning to Bombay to be reunited with her parents, instead Sarika Maynesfield found that her life was being firmly taken over by Sean O'Conner—which didn't suit her at all. And there didn't seem any way she could get rid of him...

A MOMENT IN TIME

BY
YVONNE WHITTAL

MILLS & BOON LIMITED
15–16 BROOK'S MEWS
LONDON W1A 1DR

All the characters in this book have no existence outside the imagination of the Author, and have no relation whatsoever to anyone bearing the same name or names. They are not even distantly inspired by any individual known or unknown to the Author, and all the incidents are pure invention.

The text of this publication or any part thereof may not be reproduced or transmitted in any form or by any means, electronic or mechanical, including photocopying, recording storage in an information retrieval system, or otherwise without the written permission of the publisher.

This book is sold subject to the condition that it shall not, by way of trade or otherwise, be lent, resold, hired out or otherwise circulated without the prior consent of the publisher in any form of binding or cover other than that in which it is published and without a similar condition including this condition being imposed on the subsequent purchaser.

*First published in Great Britain 1985
by Mills & Boon Limited*

© Yvonne Whittal 1985

*Australian copyright 1985
Philippine copyright 1986
This edition 1986*

ISBN 0 263 75285 2

*Set in Monophoto Times 11 on 11 pt.
01-0286 – 50456*

*Made and printed in Great Britain by
Richard Clay (The Chaucer Press) Ltd,
Bungay, Suffolk*

AUTHOR'S NOTE

Although there are many myths and legends amongst the Black peoples of southern Africa, the legend of Indlovukazi is fictitious, but the belief of her subjects, that she obtained her children through supernatural powers, is based loosely on facts which relate to the Rain Queen (Rain Goddess) of the Lobedu who reside in the Letaba district, Kruger National Park.

Y.W.

CHAPTER ONE

THE buff-coloured envelope bore the official stamp of the university. Christie Olson held it between slender fingers that shook slightly. She was anxious to know its contents, but for some obscure reason she was also a little afraid. She did not need this job with the desperate urgency of some of the other applicants, but accompanying a group of archaeological students on an expedition for the duration of a month had seemed like a challenge to brighten what had become a rather dull existence for her as secretary at a firm of accountants in Johannesburg.

Sammy Peterson had been the first to notice her restlessness. 'You have buried yourself behind a typewriter for three years, and you're too stubborn to admit that you have made a mistake,' he said a few nights ago when he had taken her out to dinner. 'What you need is the excitement of the stage and a few gruelling, but rewarding hours in a recording studio.'

Christie's generous mouth had curved in a cynical smile, but it had been wasted on the stout little man with the bald head who had sat puffing at his cigar with relish. He was accustomed to what he had termed the 'theatrical tantrums' of the artists under contract to him, and Sammy still considered Christie as his exclusive property, even though her contract had expired three years ago.

'You never give up, do you?' she had remarked wryly, raising long dark lashes to survey him with hyacinth-blue eyes, conveying an accusation which Sammy placidly ignored.

'Are you forgetting that I found you strumming your guitar and singing for a pittance in a coffee bar?' He had leaned towards her, a cloud of cigar smoke surrounding him as he fixed pale grey eyes on her. 'I made you a *star*, Christie, and now you expect me to sit back and watch you throw away everything I helped you build up with such care.'

'The choice was mine, Sammy.'

'You were emotionally unstable when you decided to quit, and I blame Lyle Venniker for that.'

'We will not discuss Lyle.' Her face had become a cold, rigid mask behind which she had hidden her feelings for five long years, and Sammy Peterson knew her well enough to realise that he had gone too far in his eagerness to lure her back into his clutches, but he was not a man to relinquish a battle when he wanted something desperately enough.

'I have a new contract typed out and waiting for you,' he had said later that night when he had left her at her flat. 'If you change your mind you know that all you have to do is come in and sign it.'

Christie had not answered him, and the following day she had gone for that interview at the university, but Sammy's words had continued to linger uncomfortably in her mind. He had made her recall that first year after she had left the orphanage to go out into the world on her own. She had been incapable of finding something to do which would provide her with an income and, out of sheer desperation, she had finally taken a job at a coffee bar, serving customers by day, and singing at night to provide herself with that little extra she had needed so badly. It was true that she did, at times, yearn for the excitement of the stage and the thrill of cutting a new record, but the price she had paid for recognition had been too high. When her contract had expired she had put that part of her life behind her, and she had vowed never to return to it.

The envelope crackled between Christie's agitated fingers. The past was something she had been determined never to dwell on, and she dragged her thoughts forcibly to the present as she ripped open the envelope and extracted a single sheet of paper. Her glance skimmed over the first few lines and her face lit up with an inner excitement. She had got the job! For a few moments she was too shaky to take in the remainder of the letter, and she simply stood there staring at it in a dazed fashion. She had never imagined that she would be successful. The other applicants had appeared more suited to an archaeological expedition, and also so much more experienced, Christie thought, when she recalled how they had rattled off their qualifications.

Christie lowered herself into a comfortable chair, and leaned back for a second with her eyes closed to calm herself sufficiently before she read the second paragraph of the letter in her hand.

'The professor and his party of students wish to leave Johannesburg on the 17th February, and it is therefore imperative that you contact us as soon as possible to discuss the final details.'

It was ironic. Lyle had once wanted her to accompany him to the excavation site of the ruined city of Pompeii in Italy, but she had been forced to decline because of her commitments elsewhere. Now, instead of Lyle, she would be accompanying a lecturing archaeologist and his small group of students on a trip to the northern Transvaal, and there was a pang of bitterness inside her at the thought.

Lyle. She did not want to think of Lyle Venniker, but the memories came crowding in on her mind with the sudden eruption of a highveld storm. They had met after a show at the home of mutual friends, and Christie had been instantly attracted to the tall, lean archaeologist with the piercing dark eyes. The attraction had been mutual, or so she had believed at the time, and a month later they had been married, despite Sammy Peterson's protestations that it was too soon. She had been twenty, starry-eyed with success, and desperately in love for the first time in her life, but her happiness had been brief. Lyle had been fiercely possessive, and he had made no secret of the fact that he had disliked the demands her career placed on her time. He had insisted that she accompany him to Italy, and Christie had been torn between her love for her husband, and her loyalty to Sammy Peterson who had given her a chance in life. Instead of understanding her predicament, Lyle had forced her to choose between him, and her career as a singer. The choice had been cruel and totally unfair. Her contract with Sammy Peterson's company had still had two years to go before it elapsed, she had been booked for recording sessions, and Sammy had had an extensive tour of the country lined up for her which could not be cancelled. There had been no way she could have escaped her commitments and, after six short, stormy months, her marriage had crumbled. The divorce had been almost as swift as their marriage. Lyle had gone to Italy alone and, to the best of her knowledge, he had never returned.

Christie shook herself free of these thoughts. After five years the pain could still bite as deep as it had on that day when Lyle had stormed out of their flat and, as she slid the letter back into its envelope, her eyes were shadowed pools of anguish best forgotten...

She sighed and got to her feet. It was getting dark outside, and she switched on the lights in her spacious and graciously furnished flat. She had always worked sparingly with her money and, after a poverty-stricken childhood, she could now afford to surround herself with the few luxuries she had accumulated over the years. There was, however, nothing ostentatious about the furnishings, and she had succeeded in creating a cool, serene, and comfortable atmosphere in whites and pastels.

Christie made herself something to eat in the kitchen before indulging in a leisurely, scented bath. She watched television for a while, but she could not concentrate on the programme and decided instead to have an early night. She would take a drive out to the university in the morning to discuss the final arrangements, and then she would have to make use of the few days left to her to go out shopping for suitable clothes. They would be camping out in tents in a place which, she had gathered, was nowhere near civilisation, and the clothes in her wardrobe were not at all suited to the kind of life she would be leading during the coming weeks.

The mirror against the wall captured the slender, supple grace of her movements when she entered the bedroom, but Christie seldom paused long enough to admire herself. She was of the opinion that her eyes were too big and her mouth too wide, and she completely overlooked the fact that, coupled with her classic bone structure, she possessed a haunting beauty which men found intensely appealing. There should have been no need for a lack of male company, but, since her divorce from Lyle, Christie had adopted a cool, aloof manner which only Sammy Peterson had succeeded in penetrating. She had been hurt once, and she had no intention of being hurt again.

The taxi driver dumped Christie's large shoulder bag on the pavement at her feet while she dipped her fingers into her purse. She paid him the required amount plus a substantial tip, and he drove away, leaving her standing alone on the campus grounds. It was a hot February morning, and after a hectic week of preparations she could already feel herself begin to wilt in the heat.

A Microbus, two large trucks, and a Jeep were parked a little distance from her. Christie smiled inwardly. She had arrived at the correct venue, there was no doubt about that, and her glance skidded towards a group of students sitting in a circle beneath a shady oak. They were discussing the planned expedition, and their obvious excitement was infectious. It made Christie's pulse-rate quicken as she picked up her heavy shoulder bag, and she was beginning to think she had gone unnoticed when a dark-haired young man detached himself from the group. He came striding towards her, and she was not unaware of the way his green glance flicked appreciatively over her slim figure clad in denims and cotton shirt.

'You must be Miss Olson,' he greeted her with a friendly smile.

'That's correct,' she confirmed, the corners of her mouth lifting in an involuntary response.

'I'm Dennis de Villiers.' Her hand was gripped and pumped up and down in an enthusiastic welcome. 'If you give me your bag I'll put it on the truck for you with the rest of our stuff. The professor should be here any moment now.'

Christie's bag was lifted off her shoulder and on to his before she could protest, and she resignedly allowed herself this final luxury. From this moment onwards she would be responsible for her own kit, regardless of its weight.

'You're very kind,' she murmured as she followed Dennis de Villiers towards the vehicles parked close by.

'Think nothing of it.' He brushed aside her remark as he dumped her bag on the back of one of the trucks, then he gestured with an inclination of his head towards the students who were now observing them curiously. 'Come along and meet the others.'

Christie was introduced to fifteen students, three of whom were young women, but it was the girl, Erica, who attracted Christie's instant attention. Fair-haired and tawny-eyed, she had a tigerish look about her that made Christie raise her guard at once.

'I'm sure you must have gathered that we're all on first name terms,' Dennis smiled, turning eagerly to Christie. 'What's yours?'

'Christie,' she answered, but she regretted it the next instant when she glimpsed a spark of intense interest in Erica's tawny eyes.

'There was a folk singer some years ago who

called herself Christie. My brother was crazy about her and bought all her records.'

'Really?' Christie adopted a bored expression to match her casual remark, but Erica was not put off.

'Don't know what happened to her, though.' She continued her subtle probing. 'She simply disappeared off the scene.'

'Perhaps her popularity waned.' Christie put forward a suggestion which she hoped would end this particular topic of conversation.

'That's hardly likely!' Erica announced with a bark of disbelieving laughter while she studied Christie intently, her glance sliding from the short, golden-brown curls framing Christie's face down to her comfortable canvas shoes. 'My brother considered her one of *the* best female country singers in southern Africa, and he should know, considering that he works at the recording company who used to produce her records.'

Christie felt a discomfiting chill spiral through her, but the conversation was ended abruptly when Dennis said excitedly, 'Here comes the professor.'

Christie turned to follow the direction of his gaze, and everything within her ground to a petrified halt. The man walking towards them with those long, lithe strides was Lyle Venniker, and past and present came together with a shattering force that rocked the secure little world Christie had created for herself during the past five years. She stood like a statue, her face chalk-white, while everyone else went forward to crowd around him, and it was only when those dark, piercing eyes met hers above the heads of the students that her heart thudded uncomfortably back to life. He uttered an abrupt command which sent the students racing towards the vehicles, and only then did he approach Christie. Never before had she felt such a fierce desire to flee from someone, but her legs refused to move, and she stood there frozen until he paused less than a pace away from her to tower over her menacingly.

Tall, lean, and tanned, he still looked the same except for a distinguished smattering of grey against his temples which made him appear a fraction older than his thirty-eight years, but there were differences which she began to notice as the numbness of shock began to ease out of her mind. The hawk-like features were sharper, the eyes harder, and the mouth sterner than she had remembered. It heightened his masculine appeal in some strange way, and Christie felt an unwanted stirring inside her when his stabbing glance lingered briefly on her hair which, five years ago, had trailed almost down to her waist.

'Fate must find a diabolical pleasure in making our paths cross once again, but I want you to know that, had I known yesterday what I discovered only this morning, I would have insisted they find someone else.'

His deep, familiar voice was harsh with biting displeasure, and Christie was roused to an icy anger she had not felt in years. 'I can assure you that I would have withdrawn my application at once had I known you would be leading this expedition.'

'Since we understand each other on that score, there are one or two matters I wish to discuss with you before we leave the campus this morning.' His manner was authoritative, and there was something close to a threat in his voice. 'The next four weeks are going to be strenuous for all of us, so don't expect any favours. Besides taking down the data and typing it, I shall expect you to help with the chores like everyone else in the camp. The group as a whole will have the opportunity to display their culinary abilities, and that rule also applies to you.'

Christie felt indignant at the deliberate insult. How dare he imagine that she would shy away from the suggestion of hard work! Her temper rose sharply, but she kept it in check, and asked coldly, 'Was there anything else?'

'Yes!' he barked, his shoulders moving beneath his blue shirt as if the material spanned too tightly across their width. 'You had better be as good at your job as they said you would be.'

If that was a challenge, then she was not going to ignore it. 'In which vehicle shall I be travelling?'

'You'll be in the first truck with Dennis de Villiers.'

'Thank you.' They glared at each other in silence for several stormy seconds. 'May I go now?'

Christie had snapped the query, and he had inclined his dark head briefly before turning and striding towards the Jeep. She stared after him for a moment, taking in those long, muscled legs in khaki trousers, the lean hips, and the wide shoulders. It seemed quite impossible to believe that they had once been so intimately close. He was now a stranger to her, and yet her mind was suddenly crowded with memories of intimacies shared that did not bear thinking about. Five years ago she had been forced to thrust him from her mind and her heart, and she had believed that she had succeeded, but seeing him today had brought back the reality of those six months when they had lived together. It had been six months of love and laughter until their differing professions had driven a wedge so deeply between them that nothing short of a miracle would have saved their marriage.

Christie shrugged off her thoughts and walked briskly towards the truck where Dennis de Villiers was seated behind the wheel. She climbed up into the cab beside him and, still smarting from Lyle's insults, she slammed the door with unnecessary force.

'Hey!' Dennis looked startled to see her there and jerked his thumb over his shoulder. 'The girls are supposed to travel in the Microbus.'

'I was told to come here, and that arrangement suits me fine.'

'The professor must be going loony!' Dennis exploded. 'You can't ride in this shuddering contraption.'

'Leave it!' The sharpness in her voice prevented him from getting out of the truck to confront Lyle. 'I shall be quite comfortable here with you.'

She had a nasty, growing suspicion that Lyle had planned to make life difficult and uncomfortable for her during the coming weeks, and instructing her to travel in this truck was merely the beginning. She forced a smile to her unwilling lips, but the uncertainty in Dennis's green gaze did not waver.

'I'll leave it if you say so, but——' The roar of a red Triumph interrupted him as it shot past the truck, and they both turned their heads to see the car come to a screeching halt in front of Lyle's Jeep. 'It looks as if we're going to be held up a while longer,' Dennis observed with a hint of impatience in his voice.

The woman who stepped out of the Triumph

was tall, fair, and strikingly beautiful, even at a distance. She walked swiftly towards the Jeep, and Lyle turned to greet her with a smile that softened his features miraculously. The woman drew down his head to kiss him on his cheek, and Christie felt a stab of something she did not wish to analyse at that moment.

'Is she joining us?' Christie asked, holding her breath for some unaccountable reason.

'Not *that* lady!' Dennis laughed derisively. 'She wouldn't soil her lily-white hands to do anything for herself, let alone for someone else.'

Christie could not take her eyes off the elegantly dressed young woman who was involved in what appeared to be a serious and involved discussion with Lyle. 'Who is she?'

'Sonia Deacon,' Dennis answered abruptly. 'Her old man is some big shot in the mines, and she latched on to the professor almost as soon as he set foot in this country six months ago.'

Dennis had unknowingly given Christie more information than she had asked for, but it was not Lyle she was concerned with at that moment. Sonia Deacon seemed to be pleading with Lyle, but his expression was unrelenting and resolute as he shook his head.

'She appears to be upset about something,' Christie remarked almost to herself.

'She's a very possessive lady, and my guess is she doesn't like the idea of the professor going away for a month and leaving her behind.'

Christie stared at Lyle's impassive features. He was listening, but he was not contributing to the conversation at that moment, and Sonia Deacon finally spun on her heel and stormed towards her car. The Triumph pulled away from the curb and

Sonia made a U-turn on screeching tyres before she shot off in the direction she had come a few minutes earlier.

Christie and Dennis exchanged glances briefly without saying anything, and the next moment they saw Lyle striding towards their truck with his dark brows drawn together in an angry frown.

'Let's go!' he barked up at Dennis. 'We've been delayed long enough!'

Lyle did not wait for Dennis to reply, but stepped back in the road and gestured with his arms to the vehicles behind them that they were preparing to leave, and a few minutes later they were turning on to the freeway to Pretoria.

Dennis had not been joking when he had called the truck a 'shuddering contraption'. The seat was hard, every bump in the road jolting her, and the heat in the cab became almost unbearable as they travelled farther north. Lyle led the convoy at a steady, even pace, and it seemed to Christie as if they had travelled for days instead of a few hours when they stopped at Potgietersrus for lunch. She deliberately sought out the company of the three young women in the group in her attempt to avoid Lyle, and she found that her initial fears about Erica subsided swiftly. She was a bright, pleasant girl, and Christie could say the same for Sandra and Valerie.

The restaurant was a cool haven after the hours of travelling in the heat, but all too soon they had to continue on their journey, and Christie reluctantly stepped out into the blazing sunlight.

'Mike will change places with you,' Valerie told Christie, tossing her red head in the direction of a sandy-haired young man leaning against the Microbus while smoking a cigarette. 'He will travel the rest of the way in the truck, and that means there will be room for you with us.'

Christie was on the point of agreeing to Valerie's suggestion when her glance collided with Lyle's, and the look on his face told her that he had heard every word Valerie had said. Derision twisted his mouth and a challenge glittered in his eyes as he waited for her to reply, and Christie had to clamp down on her temper yet again.

'Thanks for the offer,' she said to Valerie without lowering her voice, 'but I don't think we should alter the arrangements. Professor Venniker doesn't appear to be in a very good mood, and I'm quite sure he is capable of breathing the devil's own fire at us.'

Sandra was the most timid of the three female students, and she looked visibly distressed when she glanced beyond Christie and whispered, 'The professor heard you, I'm sure.'

Christie felt like saying, 'So what!', but instead she adopted a casual stance and said, 'Do you think so?'

Sandra nodded her dark head, and the next instant Lyle's deep voice barked an instruction directly behind Christie.

'Everyone in their places, we're leaving!' Christie turned towards the first truck, but fingers of steel bit briefly into her arm and forced her to face the man who stood glowering down at her. 'Any more derogatory remarks about me to the students, and I send you packing back to Johannesburg,' he instructed, his voice lowered and gratingly harsh.

The antagonism was rife between them, and for one brief moment Christie thought, This is my chance to get away, but for some inexplicable reason she heard herself murmuring an apology.

Those familiar dark eyes burned down into hers for a moment before he turned on his heel and walked on ahead towards the Jeep. Christie had no desire to draw attention to herself, and she followed him hastily. She climbed up into the truck beside Dennis, but she was fuming inwardly, and she was glaring at Lyle without realising it when he eased his lean length into the Jeep.

The truck shuddered to life beneath Christie when Dennis turned the key in the ignition and when the Jeep pulled away from the curb, Dennis followed suit.

'The professor's not such a bad guy once you get to know him,' Dennis remarked without taking his eyes off the road, and Christie realised with a start that he must have overheard the remark she had passed earlier.

'I'm sure you're right,' she answered stiffly, but she warned herself silently that she would have to exercise more care in future if she did not want the students to suspect that she had known Lyle before their meeting that morning. 'I've never been a good traveller, and the heat has made me snappish,' she excused her behaviour, and she was not being altogether untruthful.

'It's been a tough day.' Dennis acknowledged her explanation, and after that they lapsed into a silence which Christie welcomed.

They left the national road and took a secondary road in a north-westerly direction. Christie had never travelled this far north before, and she was amazed at how the vegetation changed. They had left the mountains behind them, but the road they travelled seemed to rise over hills and dip down into valleys where the vegetation was green and fertile along the banks of the rivers and their tributaries.

It was becoming stiflingly hot. Her throat felt parched, and her clothes were beginning to cling uncomfortably to her damp body. One glance at Dennis told her that he was feeling the heat as much as she. The perspiration was running freely down her face and neck, and his shirt was damp with sweat under the armpits.

'How far do we still have to go?' Christie questioned him, pushing her dark glasses up into her hair and wiping her face with a handkerchief.

'Another fifty kilometres, I think.'

Christie sighed inwardly, and wondered if her tortured spine would ever be the same again. Fifty kilometres was nothing on a decent highway, but they had turned on to a gravel road some time ago to travel in a cloud of dust kicked up by the Jeep in front of them. One glance through the rear window told Christie that the truck was kicking up an even bigger cloud of dust, and she felt a great deal more sympathy for those in the vehicles behind them.

It was mid-afternoon before they reached Dialsdrif. It was a small town with no more than a half-dozen shops, and a smattering of quaint little houses nestling amongst honeysuckle hedges and shady trees. The Jeep slowed down when they entered the town, and Dennis put his foot on the brake pedal to do the same. Christie had thought that they would travel through the town without stopping, but Lyle signalled them all to a halt near the shops.

No one needed a second invitation to ease their aching bodies out of the dusty vehicles to stretch their legs. Christie had never before seen such a travel-weary group of people huddled together on a pavement, but when she glanced at Lyle she found him to be the exception. She had always admired him for that surplus amount of energy and vitality he seemed to possess, and she could not help but admire him now as he leapt out of the Jeep to come striding towards them. Everyone else had wilted hours ago, but Lyle still looked almost as fresh as when they had left the campus grounds early that morning.

'This is the last town before we leave civilization behind us, and after this someone will be coming in to Dialsdrif once a week only to replenish supplies and to get whatever else we may need.' His dark gaze swept over them, rested for one brief, impersonal moment on Christie, and then darted away again. 'If any of you have thought of something you might need and didn't bring with you, then I suggest you get it now. You have thirty minutes, no more.' he added, glancing at his wristwatch.

'I could do with something cold to drink,' Dennis said beside Christie. 'How about you?'

'I've been almost dying of thirst for simply ages,' she admitted, turning towards the trading store which appeared to sell everything from a safety pin to large farming implements.

'Christina!' Christie froze, and it took a moment before she could control her features sufficiently to turn and face Lyle. He had never called her Christina, not even during moments of anger, and the sound of her baptismal name on his lips made her feel oddly as if she had been thrust out into the cold. She shivered despite the heat of the scorching sun, and forced herself to meet his piercing glance. 'Did you bring a hat with you?'

She was not certain what she had expected, but his query surprised her into a state of confusion. 'No, I—I——'

'I suggest you buy one.' He interrupted her faltering reply in a brusque voice. 'The sun can get dangerously hot in this part of the country.'

It felt as if the dust on the pavement had settled in her throat, and the brief touch of his hand against the hollow of her back seemed to burn her through her shirt when he ushered her into the store. He did not linger at her side, as she had feared he might, but strode towards the windowed refrigerator to help himself to a canned fruit drink.

Invaded by the students, the store shrank considerably in size, but Christie was conscious only of Lyle at that moment, and the burning touch of his hand which still seemed to linger against her back. Did he actually care that she might get sunstroke, or was he merely attempting to avoid the possibility of being inconvenienced? She shrugged slightly as she selected at random a wide-brimmed straw hat and a fruit drink for which she paid the lean, grey-haired man behind the counter. She could feel Lyle's dark eyes following every movement she made, and she walked out of the shop to escape his disquieting observation of her, but he followed her after a brief interval to where she stood leaning against the stem of a tree which cast shade on to the pavement.

Christie tried to ignore him. She snapped open the can and drank her fruit drink thirstily, but Lyle was not the type of man one could simply ignore. He made his presence acutely felt as he stood directly in front of her with his hands resting casually on his lean hips, but there was nothing casual about the way he was looking at her. His eyes were systematically stripping her down to her skin in a deliberate attempt to insult and humiliate her ... and he succeeded. An embarrassing warmth surged from her throat into her face, and for some ridiculous reason she wanted to cry, but anger came quickly to her rescue. It was years since Lyle had caused her to shed tears, and she was not going to start again now simply because he had succeeded in making her feel like a disgusting little insect which had dared to crawl out from under a stone at his feet.

'What happened to your fabulous career?' His smile stressed the sarcasm in his query, and Christie bit back an equally sarcastic reply when she glimpsed a party of students emerging from the door.

'My contract expired three years ago,' she heard herself confiding in him without actually intending to. 'I had lost interest in a career as a singer, so I enrolled at a secretarial college, and finally found myself a job that didn't require being in the limelight.'

'I seem to recall that you thrived on being the centre of attraction.'

'That remark proves that you didn't know me at all.'

They glared at each other not for the first time that day, and she saw again that little muscle jerking along the side of his jaw to indicate that he was furious.

'Why the devil did you have to apply for this job?' he demanded in a low, frightening growl.

Christie shrugged with a casualness she did not feel. 'It's different to anything I have ever done before, and it sounded adventurous.'

'The students are not here for the adventure,' he warned in a harsh undertone, and he was standing so close that she could detect the familiar and tantalising odour of his masculine cologne. 'This expedition is a vital and enriching part of their studies, and you would do well to remember that.'

Christie was surprised to discover that she was shaking when he strode away from her. She had never before had cause to fear Lyle, but she feared him now. She sensed an unfamiliar violence in him which she had not encountered during their brief marriage, and she actually found herself dreading the four weeks ahead of her as his secretary. He was going to be an extremely difficult employer, and exactly *how* difficult she was yet to find out.

CHAPTER TWO

THE camp site was midway between a rugged, sloping mountain with a rocky ridge running along its crest, and the Mogalakwena River. It was ideal, for both were situated within five minutes' walking distance from the camp, and their first day was spent acquainting themselves with their new environment. Erica, Sandra, and Valerie shared a tent, and the men shared three tents between them. Christie had a tent to herself, and she could not decide whether it was intended for her to feel privileged, or isolated from the rest of the group. Lyle also had a large tent to himself which was partitioned off to serve as an office as well as sleeping quarters.

A sharp bend in the Mogalakwena River, aided by a natural outcrop of rocks, created a shallow pool in which it was safe for them to bathe, and they had brought sufficient water for drinking and cooking purposes to last them a week. Perishable food was kept in a gas refrigerator in the supply tent, and their meals were cooked on a gas stove and an open fire. It was all very organised and considerably more civilised than Christie had imagined it would be, but she nevertheless found it strange eating out under the stars with the unfamiliar night sounds providing a primitive and rather frightening atmosphere. Exhaustion had driven everyone to bed early that first night, but it had taken Christie quite a time to fall asleep. The sleeping bag and stretcher were poor substitutes for the comfortable bed in her Johannesburg flat, and in the silent darkness of her small tent it felt as if she was the only living soul left on earth. She had been afraid that she might lie awake most of the night, but she had finally drifted into a dreamless sleep from which she had been awakened at first light the following morning.

Excavations began on the second day beneath the rocky face of the mountain, where a natural cave bore indications that it might once have been inhabited by one of the many ancient African tribes. The equipment was carried laboriously up the steep slope of the mountain. The site was marked off in squares, and a precise diagram was made for the purpose of marking the exact spot where a specimen was found. *If* anything was ever found, Christie added sceptically to herself.

Armed with a notebook and pencil, and dressed in comfortable canvas shoes, denims and a cotton shirt, Christie had followed the group up the mountain. If she had expected that she would simply be taking down notes, then she was mistaken. Lyle issued cryptic instructions to everyone, and Christie found herself working alongside him to assist with the rigging of some of the equipment before the excavations could begin.

As the morning progressed the heat and the humidity shot up several discomforting degrees, and they all were made to realise why Lyle had worn shorts instead of slacks, and a T-shirt which he stripped off eventually to leave his muscled torso exposed to the sun. The male students followed his example, and stripped off their shirts, but the girls had to suffer in silence.

'I'm wearing shorts tomorrow and my bikini

top,' Erica declared emphatically when they returned to the camp for lunch, and Christie and the other two girls agreed with her.

They did not return to the excavation site in the afternoon. They gathered together in the shade of a weeping wattle, discussing the morning's activities, and this, in itself, took the form of a lecture. The students asked questions and made frequent notes of what they considered important, and afterwards they dispersed, leaving Christie alone with Lyle.

She felt nervous and edgy, and not quite certain what was expected of her. She fiddled with her notebook and pencil, and tried not to look at him, but her glance was irrevocably drawn to his naked torso where the dark hair on his wide chest tapered down to his navel. His maleness was as potent now as it had been five years ago, and her response to it was unexpected and alarming. Her insides trembled and her palms felt clammy when she rose jerkily to her feet. Memories flooded her mind, memories of her cheek resting against his hair-roughened chest, and her heart pounded wildly in her breast at the intimate trend of her thoughts. She wondered if he could recall as much about her as she could about him, but his dark eyes were devoid of any emotion except that biting displeasure that made her cringe inwardly.

'Where do you think you're going?' Lyle demanded when she turned from him to escape to her tent, and her body stiffened as she stopped and turned to face him again with a practised calmness.

'Do you need me for anything?' she counter-questioned.

Lyle rose slowly from the low canvas stool, and

he stood towering over her in a way that made her feel threatened and on the defensive. 'There's work to be done.'

He strode ahead of her towards his tent, and Christie followed at a slower, rather uncertain pace. She had kept her notebook and pencil handy, feeling her way around rather more than being told what to do. She had made notes that morning, taking down everything and anything which she had thought might be of importance, and she soon had cause to refer to those notes. Lyle gestured her into a chair, and started dictating technical data at a speed which made it almost impossible for her to keep up with him, but she gave no outward indication of her discomfort.

'Read that back to me,' he snapped much later when he came to the end of a sentence, and Christie did so at once without stumbling until she encountered something which seemed to contradict the information she had jotted down that morning.

'You said this morning that the history of southern Africa dates back only to the seventeenth century,' she voiced her confusion, 'but now you're saying that it goes back a million years.'

'That's quite correct.' He lowered his lean length into a canvas chair and lit a cigarette. 'The known history of southern Africa dates back to the seventeenth century when the first literate settlers and explorers began to write about this country, and what they found and did here, but it is an archaeologist's task to discover the prehistory and to reconstruct the activities of man in prehistoric times.'

'Oh.' Christie was convinced that she looked as foolish as she felt, but she recovered swiftly, and turned the situation to her advantage. 'Do you expect to find anything of interest?'

'There's always the possibility that we might, but the owner of this property thinks we're wasting our time.'

A smile had softened his stern, hawk-like features for the briefest second while he spoke, and yet another layer of ice melted around her heart. She knew the danger of thawing emotionally. It would open doors she had been determined would remain locked for ever, and it would release the pain she had known once before.

'How will it affect the students if their efforts turn out to be fruitless?' she asked, shutting her mind to everything except her growing interest in this project.

'It shouldn't affect them in any way at all.' His dark eyes observed her through a screen of smoke, and mocked her for her concern. 'They will have gained invaluable practical experience, and that's the most important reason for this expedition.'

'I see.' She was feeling foolish again, and she lowered her gaze hastily to the notebook she clutched in her hands.

'Any further questions?' he queried abruptly.

'No,' she shook her head, her golden-brown curls changing to warm honey in the shaft of sunlight as they danced about her face.

'Then I suggest that you continue where you left off.'

'Sorry,' she gulped at the censorious rebuke in his voice, and for the next five minutes she concentrated solely on reading aloud the information she had taken down in shorthand.

The silence that followed was disturbed only by the sound of the birds in the trees, and the laughter of the students. They were as keyed-up with excitement as Christie was with nerves and, when she risked an upward glance, her hyacinth-blue eyes widened at the angry intensity of Lyle's dark gaze.

'Why are you looking at me like that?' she asked, the mellowness of her voice husky with tension.

Lyle crushed the remainder of his cigarette into a metal ashtray, and rose to his feet. There was a smouldering fury in his actions, and it was evident in the flames that leapt in his eyes when they blazed down into hers.

'There was a time when I would have given anything for you to accompany me on an expedition.'

'And now I suddenly arrive on the scene like a toothache you would rather do without,' Christie finished for him with a cynicism forced on her by pain and suffering. 'Is that what you're trying to say?'

'That's it exactly!'

It felt as if a heavy weight had lodged in Christie's chest, and her throat tightened on a not unfamiliar ache. 'Do you hate me that much?'

'What I feel for you is total indifference,' he lashed her verbally. 'What I *hate* is raking the dead past back into the present.'

Total indifference. The dead past. That hurt! It ripped at wounds she had imagined healed, and it took a concentrated effort to control her features in an attempt to disguise her pain.

'That's an odd remark coming from an archaeologist such as yourself,' she mocked him openly.

'I was speaking personally, not professionally, and you damn well know that!'

It felt as if the heat in the tent was beginning to suffocate her as she stared up into his furious face, and she marvelled at the stranger Lyle had become. 'I suppose it hadn't occurred to you that I might find the existing situation equally unpleasant?'

'I don't doubt that you do, but there is no harm in stressing my feelings on the matter to ensure that we survive the next four weeks.' Authoritative and commanding even without a shirt, he surveyed her disdainfully. 'You will find whatever stationery you may require in that box under the table. Type an original plus two copies of the notes I have given you, and leave it in that green file on the table.'

'Yes, Professor,' she replied mockingly and—she had to admit—with a certain amount of awe, but her form of address drew a furious scowl from Lyle before he walked out the tent and left her alone.

Total indifference. The dead past. The words spilled cruelly back into her mind to remain locked there in a mad crescendo. She had built up an armour over the years which she had believed would shut out pain, but those words had pierced her armour like a hot knife slicing through butter. *Damn* Lyle Venniker for coming back into her life, and *damn* him for striking her where it hurt most. She could have tolerated his displeasure, even his hatred, but indifference from Lyle was like a bad taste in the mouth which not even the most expensive mouthwash could rid you of.

She thrust these thoughts forcefully from her mind, and got up to pull the cover off the small typewriter. In the box under the low, fold-up table she found the necessary typing paper and carbon, and she pulled the chair closer to the table before she sat down. It took a few seconds to acquaint herself with the typewriter, and after that she became immersed in typing out the notes Lyle had given her.

It was hot inside the tent despite the fact that the flap at the entrance had been raised on poles to create a shady verandah. Not a breeze stirred through the bushveld that afternoon to cool the tent, and she perspired freely until her cotton shirt clung to her skin. Her hands felt clammy, but her fingers moved rapidly over the keys, and an hour later she pulled the last sheet of paper out of the typewriter. Christie was aware again of the activity in the camp, and then the sound of footsteps made her turn to see Dennis entering the tent.

'We're all going down to the river for a swim,' he said, his green glance taking in her hot face and damp shirt. 'Wouldn't you like to join us?'

Nothing would have given her more pleasure than to plunge her heated body into cool water, but she still had to read through her work to check for typing errors, and she shook her head ruefully. 'I'm sorry, Dennis, but I still have quite a bit of work to do.'

'Oh, come on, Christie.' He brushed aside her excuse. 'I'm sure the professor wouldn't mind if you took a short break in this heat.'

'Your judgment is incorrect, Dennis.' Christie spun round on her chair at the sound of Lyle's voice, and one look at his face was enough to make her feel like an errant teenager instead of a woman of twenty-five. 'Please keep in mind that Miss Olson is here in a working capacity, and not for the purpose of indulging in a paid holiday.'

'But, Professor——'

'And neither is she here for your entertainment,' Lyle interrupted Dennis cuttingly.

'Professor, I wasn't——'

'That will be all!' Lyle cut in once again.

A mixture of surprise and annoyance flashed across Dennis's face, but it was swiftly concealed before he turned away and joined the party of students strolling down to the river.

Christie regretted the incident. It was not fair on Dennis that Lyle should have taken his anger out on him, and she leapt to the young man's defence. 'Don't be too harsh on him, he was merely——'

'I don't need you to instruct me how to deal with the students,' Lyle barked at her before she could complete her sentence, and her anger rose sharply.

'It wasn't my intention to interfere, but if you want to take your bad temper out on someone, then I suggest you take it out on me, and not Dennis for showing me a little kindness and consideration.'

'This is not a benevolence society,' he countered harshly. 'You are here to work normal office hours, but what you do during your free time is your affair entirely.'

'Oh, so I *am* going to have a little free time, am I?' she demanded with icy sarcasm, but she regretted her attitude when she saw his eyes narrow to slits of fury.

'Keep a civil tongue in your head when you speak to me, Christina Olson,' he warned, his voice low and threatening as he leaned over her with one hand on the back of her chair and the other on the table, imprisoning her. 'If you undermine my authority with the students I shan't be held responsible for my actions.'

Instinct warned her to take care, but a little demon inside her drove her on, and she smiled up at him cynically. 'What will you do, Professor Venniker? Thrash me?'

The dark eyes flashed a fire that seemed to scorch her. 'I might just do that if you're not careful.'

'How strange that I never noticed this streak of violence in you before.' She continued to taunt him mockingly as that demon inside her drove her beyond the limit of caution.

Lyle's jaw hardened, and she could almost feel the fury vibrating through his body and into her chair where his hand tightened on it with a savageness that made her fear that the wood would snap. 'Drive me too far, Christie, and you'll live to regret it.'

His face was so close to hers that she could see the pores in his skin, but her mind registered more than that before he straightened and walked away from her in the direction of the river.

Christie sat there like someone stunned. Lyle was not a stranger to her, and yet she felt as if she did not know him at all. She could understand that he might have been shocked and annoyed at discovering that she was to accompany him on this trip; she had felt the same when she knew he was to be her employer, but she could not understand this deep-seated anger which seemed to emanate from him whenever he was near her. *Why?* Surely she had more right to such a fierce anger after the cruel choice he had forced her to make five years ago?

She shivered as the perspiration trickled down her back, but it was a shiver that left her cold despite the heat in the tent. Something was dreadfully wrong! Her instincts had never let her down before, and she knew she could rely on them now. Lyle could not have nurtured such a frightening anger all these years for no reason at all, and she was convinced that something must have occurred which she had no knowledge of. But *what?* She had to find out, but Lyle was the last person she could, or *would* approach in her search for the answer. Sammy Peterson? Yes, she would speak to Sammy as soon as she returned to Johannesburg ... *if* she returned in one piece after four weeks with Lyle in the wilderness.

Christie had difficulty in regaining her concentration, but she finally succeeded in reading through the typed sheets to check for errors. The remainder of the afternoon passed quickly, and she was looking forward to a refreshing swim in the river the moment she was free.

The students returned to the camp in a light-hearted mood, and Christie's glance sought Lyle. His hair was damp and lying in a disorderly manner across his forehead, and that well-remembered smile lightened his stern features. Something clutched at her heart, squeezing it until it almost ached with a feeling she was not yet ready to acknowledge, but she froze inside the moment his eyes met hers. The smile vanished from his hawk-like features, and she was once again confronted with that look which came close to hatred. The ache inside her deepened, became a stabbing blade, and she turned abruptly to place the typed sheets in the file on the table. She heard Lyle's step behind her, and felt his presence in every quivering nerve, but she could not bear to turn and face him. Her feelings were too raw at that moment; they lay naked in her eyes, and the humilitating truth hit her as she fled from him into the privacy of her own tent not far from his.

Lyle still had the power to hurt her more than anyone else on this earth and, with this knowledge, she found herself faced with the agonising truth. She had never stopped loving him. For her own preservation she had made herself believe that she hated him, but she knew now that it had been a subconscious façade. She may have succeeded in banishing him from her mind, but her heart had stubbornly refused to set him free.

Christie drew a choking breath, and the stretcher creaked protestingly beneath her weight when she sat down heavily. She stared at the ground-sheet protecting her from the dampness of the earth at night, but all she could see was Lyle's harsh, angry features, and she smothered a choked cry when she buried her white face in her hands.

Several minutes elapsed before she succeeded in controlling herself, then she left her tent, taking her soap and towel with her for that longed-for bathe in the river. But she had barely taken a half dozen paces when a harsh voice behind her demanded; 'Where do you think you're going?'

She turned slowly, forcing her features to adopt that cool, calm mask she had been forced to wear for so long, and she gestured with her towel. 'That's obvious, isn't it?'

'It's also obvious to me that you have neglected to check the roster which has been drawn up.' Christie stared at him blankly, and he gestured disparagingly before he enlightened her. 'It's your turn to assist with the evening meal.'

Hot, tired, and hurt by his attitude, she resorted to anger as her only defence. 'Surely there is time for me to have a quick wash in the river before carrying out my other duties, or would your meticulous lifestyle be inconvenienced by a delay of a few minutes?'

His face darkened with that unfathomable anger. 'I made it quite clear when we arrived here that the roster was to be stricly adhered to.'

'You made it quite clear that we would all have certain duties on certain days, and I don't object to that, but I do object to being denied the privileges you so readily grant the others. I'm not a slave who has to jump every time you crack the whip.'

'You're forgetting something,' he mocked her ruthlessly. 'I'm being paid to crack the whip, and you're being paid to jump.'

He turned on his heel and strode towards his tent, leaving her with the feeling that, if this was a battle, he had scored yet another point against her.

Christie was shaking as a storm of helpless fury raged through her. She walked back to the tent to dispose of her soap and her towel, and she found Sandra standing at the entrance with a guilty flush on her cheeks.

'I'm sorry, Christie, I didn't mean to listen in on your conversation with the professor,' she apologised as Christie brushed past her to fling her things into the tent. 'I came over for a chat, and I couldn't help hearing.'

'It doesn't matter,' Christie assured her with a calmness which belied the storm inside her.

'I can't understand why the professor is being so unreasonable where you're concerned, but I'll take your turn at the cooking this evening if you'd like to go down for a bathe,' Sandra offered generously, but Christie shook her head firmly.

'I'll leave the privilege of a bath until morning.'

A look of uncertainty flashed in Sandra's grey eyes as she studied Christie, then she walked away to join the rest of the group, leaving Christie to wash her face and hands in the basin of water in her tent before she went out to prepare the evening meal.

Mike, stockily built and sandy-haired, was Christie's partner on this occasion. He chopped the wood and stacked the fire, and proved to be a valuable assistant, stepping in when Christie found herself at a loss with this primitive method of cooking meat and vegetables.

Lyle did not come out of his tent until he was called for dinner, and Christie noticed that he had not changed out of the clothes he had worn all day except for putting on his shirt and combing his hair. Christie felt something tighten inside her, and her pulse quickened as memories flooded her mind. Lyle had always looked devastatingly attractive no matter what he had worn, and his mere presence still had the power to affect her as it had done five years ago. Her legs felt weak when he stood facing her across the narrow table, and she prayed that he would not notice the tremor in her hand when she served his food into the enamel plate he held out towards her, but the derisive smile curving his mouth told her that his razor-sharp glance had missed nothing. He knew that his presence disturbed her, and she was angry with herself for her inability to hide the fact.

A ritual was begun that evening which was to continue throughout their stay in the bushveld. The cooking utensils were washed and stacked away in the supply tent, and after that they were all free to gather around the log fire in a relaxed mood to discuss the events of that day. A tall, slender young man with red hair and freckles produced a battered guitar, and he plucked away softly at a melody which was familiar to Christie. The music would not have been disturbing if he had not made so many blatant errors, but no one other than Christie's musically toned ear seemed to hear.

'Come on, Alan, play something we can all sing to,' Dennis suggested at length, and Alan strummed boisterously as he led them into that old favourite, *Mona Lisa*.

It was with a measure of shock that Christie listened to the words of the song. Lyle had once confessed to her that her 'mystic smile' at their first meeting had made him dub her the *Mona Lisa* until, of course, they had been introduced. Did he remember? She risked a glance in his direction, but he was looking the other way, and he was obviously lost in thought to the extent that she was convinced he was unaware of the song being sung. *Damn!* she cursed silently. It was not fair that *she* remembered so much while *he* seemed oblivious of the little things which had once bound them together.

The singing was halting and hesitant as everyone stumbled over the unfamiliar lyrics of some of the songs, but Christie remained obliquely silent, not daring to participate. It was when Alan played a song which had been one of her favourites that she looked up to find Lyle's dark eyes observing her with a mocking query in their depths. For one terrible moment when the song had ended, she thought that he was going to reveal that she had been a stage and recording artist, but an odd look flashed across his face before he turned abruptly and disappeared into the shadows. Had he, perhaps, sensed her reluctance to have her past made known? Or had he correctly interpreted the silent plea in her eyes? Whatever the case, she could not suppress the sigh of relief that passed her lips when he had walked away from the happy group around the fire.

Christie did not stay up late. She said good night and left to seek out the privacy of her tent for a wash before she crawled wearily into her sleeping bag. The sound of singing voices, some toneless, did not disturb her, but she could not settle down and go to sleep. She was thinking about Lyle, about her feelings for him, and she wondered once again what had happened that could have filled him with such a terrible anger.

She repeatedly recounted in her mind those final weeks they had been together before he had left for Italy. They had argued about her commitments, which would force them to part for a time, and he had, in the end, insisted that she choose between him and her career. She had been forced to choose her career, and he had packed his bags and stormed out of their flat with the words, 'I'm not coming back, so I suggest you file for a divorce.'

Nothing else had happened; nothing, at least, that she could think of at that moment. She had waited for three months, hoping desperately that his actions had been prompted by disappointment, but her spirits had been at their lowest ebb during the fourth month after his departure. It was then that Sammy Peterson had convinced her it would be futile to go on hoping for something which would never happen. She had filed for a divorce,

Lyle had not contested it, and after some weeks she had been free of a marriage which she had once believed would last forever. She had taken back her maiden name, Olson, and Sammy had been a tower of strength during those painful months while she tried to eradicate from her mind the knowledge that she had ever known a man like Lyle Venniker.

What reason could he have for the anger which seemed to simmer like a volcano inside him? He had wanted a divorce, and she had given it to him. Why, then, did he hate her so much? *No*, she corrected herself, *he did not hate her*. He had said that what he felt for her was *total indifference*. Why did her presence anger him if he was totally indifferent?

It was hopeless trying to understand his behaviour without knowing more. Her mind was simply spinning in endless, ever-increasing circles without finding the solution, and it left her exhausted.

The camp was silent an hour later, but sleep continued to evade her, and she spent almost the entire night tossing about restlessly in her sleeping bag.

She was up before dawn the following morning, and the sun had not yet risen when she walked down to the river along a natural path among the sometimes spiky grass. It was a warm morning, and she peeled off her clothes before plunging into the cool water of the clear pool. She swam for a brief while, enjoying the refreshing feeling of the river water against her naked flesh, and it cooled her heated body at long last after a fretful night. The sun was spreading its golden, streaky glow across the dew wet earth when she reached for the cake of soap she had left on a rock with her towel, and she quickly soaped her body and washed her hair. It felt good, and she felt alive again as she lowered her body into the water to rinse off the soap before she stepped out of the water to towel herself dry and put on her clothes.

Her slender, supple body was smooth and tanned except where her bikini had protected her. Her breasts were small and firm, her legs long and shapely, but her thoughts were not concerned with her physical appearance while she zipped herself into her beige shorts and reached for her green-striped blouse. She was thinking of Lyle. She had considered herself immune, but seeing him again had served to prove her wrong. Loving him had once been a joy, but it would now be an agony. He no longer cared for her. He had made that abundantly clear while she, like an idiot, had allowed that old love to come alive again. Fate had been cruel to throw them together again after all this time, and God only knew what heartache still lay ahead of her.

Christie turned while she slipped her arms into her sleeveless blouse. Some sixth sense must have warned her that she was no longer alone, and she froze the next instant. The object of her disturbing thoughts was standing a few paces away from her with his back resting against the stem of a weeping wattle, and his arms crossed over his wide chest. Khaki shorts hugged his lean hips, accentuating the length of muscular thighs and calves, and his dark gaze wandered over her with a deliberate insolence that made her breath catch in her throat when his probing glance settled on her naked, pointed breasts. Her cheeks flamed, and she hastily dragged the two sections of her blouse together to protect herself against this onslaught. His mouth curved sensually, sending the blood pounding through her veins, and she could amost hate him at that moment for invading her privacy and placing her at an immediate disadvantage.

CHAPTER THREE

'How long have you been standing there?' demanded Christie, her voice cold with anger as she turned her back on him and fumbled the buttons of her blouse into position with shaky fingers.

'Long enough,' came the mortifying reply, while she pushed her feet into her sandals and combed her fingers through her short, damp curls.

Christie waited a moment for her colour to subside before she turned to face Lyle. 'I was given to understand that this particular pool was out of bounds to the men.'

His mocking smile deepened and his dark eyes surveyed her from head to foot in a way that made her feel naked once again. 'Where you and I are concerned that rule doesn't apply, Christina.'

'That's where you're mistaken, *Professor!*' she retorted with an icy anger that lent sparks to her eyes. 'I'm entitled to my privacy just as much as any of the other girls.'

'I find your modesty difficult to accept, and also somewhat amusing.'

'I don't see why you should,' she replied with a calmness she was far from experiencing as she picked up her things and prepared to flee.

'Oh, come now, Christie,' he laughed shortly, but there was no humour in his laugh, only a biting sarcasm. 'Do you expect me to believe that I'm the only man who has ever seen you without your clothes on?'

Christie stared at him speechlessly. His remark was a blatant insult she could not ignore no matter how much she wanted to. She tried to speak; to say something in her defence, but it felt as if her tongue had become permanently locked in her throat.

'How many men, I wonder, have had the pleasure of taking your delightful body into their beds?' he persisted with a sneer, pushing himself away from the stem of the wattle to lessen the distance between them, and it felt to Christie as if his eyes were intent upon destroying her with the fire that burned in them. 'As I recall, Sammy Peterson never could keep his fat little paws off you, and it wouldn't surprise me if he was one of your lovers.'

The blood drained from Christie's face to leave her white as a sheet. She had, at times, looked upon Sammy Peterson as the father she had never had, and he had treated her with affection, nothing more, but Lyle's remark made a wave of nausea rise inside her which she could barely suppress. Her relationship with Sammy had always been based on friendship and business, but Lyle had suddenly tainted it to a degree where it appeared dirty and vulgar.

'*You're disgusting!*' The words finally exploded in a hiss of fury from her stiff, unwilling lips.

'Am I?' An ugly smile curved Lyle's mouth. 'Let me show you how disgusting I *can* be.'

Christie was crushed against his lean, hard length before she had time to anticipate his actions, and the shock of this unexpected contact with his body sent a weakness surging into her limbs. His strong fingers gripped a handful of damp hair at the nape of her neck, forcing her white face out into the open, and his mouth clamped down on hers with a bruising force that made her moan in protest and agony against his lips. Her towel and her soap slipped from her grasp as a heavy blanket of darkness threatened to engulf her mind, but she fought against it as she felt his hands roam her body. His touch insulted her, made her feel cheap, and she worked her hands in between them in a desperate attempt to push Lyle away from her.

He released her as abruptly as he had taken her, and she staggered away from him, dazed and white-faced. She raised the back of her hand to her bruised, swollen lips, her eyes wide and dark as they met his accusingly, but his derisive smile did not waver for a moment.

'I don't deserve your insults,' she croaked in her defence, and he laughed satanically.

That was the last straw. She snatched up her things and fled, but she could not recall afterwards how she had got to her tent without stumbling and falling along the uneven, twisting path up to the camp.

Christie put her soap away and hooked up her towel to dry, but she did so automatically. She felt numb and deeply hurt, and she would have given anything to erase the memory of Lyle's hands on her body. His touch had been degrading; it had made her feel like a piece of cheap merchandise which had been handled often, and that feeling of nausea returned to leave her ashen-faced and shaking.

'Is anything wrong?' Christie spun round to see Valerie standing at the entrance to her tent with the early morning sun igniting a flame in her auburn hair. 'You looked upset when you returned to the camp a few minutes ago, and you're extremely pale.'

'I have a headache.' That was not a lie. Christie's head was pounding with renewed anger at the insults she had been forced to bear. 'It's nothing serious,' Christie lied this time, attemping a smile and failing.

'Do you have anything to take for it?' Valerie questioned her with concern in her hazel eyes. 'I'm sure the professor has a supply of headache tablets in his first-aid kit.'

'Oh, God!' Christie groaned inwardly. All she needed now was for Lyle to discover that he had upset her to the point where she needed medication!

'I have some aspirin in my haversack,' Christie assured her hastily. 'Thanks all the same.'

'Are you sure you will be okay?' Valerie persisted, obviously not entirely convinced that it was merely a headache.

'I'll be fine,' Christie insisted.

The younger girl hesitated a moment, then she turned away, saying, 'Let me know if I can get you something.'

Christie did not leave her tent until the pounding in her head had subsided. She swallowed down a couple of aspirins as a precautionary measure, and brushed her swiftly drying hair into some order. The camp was coming alive, and she could smell the sausages and eggs being prepared for breakfast on the gas stove, but she continued to linger in her tent. She studied herself in the small hand-mirror while she applied a touch of make-up. Her colour had returned almost to normal, but there was a rawness inside her that made her feel as if she had taken a physical pounding. She could hear Lyle speaking to someone a little distance from her tent, and she cringed inwardly at the thought of having to face him again. He had insulted her unfairly, and she wished that she knew the reason for it. Lyle, more than anyone else, should have known that she was not guilty of the vile insinuations he had made, but for some obscure reason he had become a demon possessed with the desire to hurt her.

Why? she wondered not for the first time. Was this his idea of taking revenge because she had been forced to place the importance of her career above that of their marriage? But why did he have this desire for revenge if he felt nothing but indifference towards her? Or was he, perhaps, not as indifferent as he wished her to believe? This was a tantalising thought, but there was no time to dwell on it. The chef for that morning was banging a ladle against a pan to indicate that breakfast was ready to be served, and Christie steeled herself for her second meeting with Lyle that morning.

She need not have been concerned. Lyle barely looked her way and, during the course of the morning, he behaved in an abrupt and impersonal manner towards her. The students were digging, sifting, and examining every particle they removed from the earth, but storm clouds had risen to obliterate the sun, and they were forced to return to the camp long before lunch that day.

The sky darkened ominously while they sat down to an early lunch, and the menacing roll of thunder drew nearer with every second. The cooking utensils had barely been packed away when the first heavy drops of rain fell. Lightning snaked unexpectedly across the darkened sky, making the air crackle with electricity, and it was followed by a clap of thunder which seemed to tear the heavens apart. The rain came down with a battering force that sent everyone dashing into their respective tents, and for the next hour Christie lay curled up on her stretcher with her pillow over her head to obliterate the frightening sound of the thunder.

The storm passed at last and, miraculously, the sun emerged to bathe the bushveld in a bright golden glow. The wet earth smelled clean and fresh when Christie walked the short distance from her tent to Lyle's, and she breathed the air deeply into her lungs. She wished that she did not have to spend the rest of the day in front of a typewriter, but, as Lyle had so brutally pointed out, she was not on a paid holiday.

Lyle was lounging in a chair with a large book on his lap when she entered his tent. He looked up, his dark glance impersonal and cold, then he waved her away. Christie stared at him stupidly. Was he actually granting her silent wish and giving her the afternoon off? Impossible!

He looked up again to find her hovering with uncertainty. 'If you're not out of here in two seconds flat I'll change my mind about giving you the afternoon off, and I'll soon find something for you to do.'

'Thanks, I'm going,' she assured him hastily, turning and walking away in a blind haste that sent her cannoning seconds later into Dennis.

'What are you running away from?' he teased, his hands on her shoulders steadying her.

'I'm running away from work,' she confessed. 'I've got the afternoon off.'

'That's great!' he smiled broadly. 'I was thinking of going for a walk to explore the area on my own, but I wouldn't object to your company.'

'If that's an invitation, then I accept,' she

answered him with a burst of light-heartedness she had not felt in ages and, linking her arm through his, they strolled out of the camp towards the area below the site which they had marked off for their excavations.

Christie's quizzical glance darted at Dennis several times. He was walking with his head lowered while she was walking with her face raised towards the sky, and a humorous smile lifted the corners of her mouth. 'Are you looking for something in particular, or do you simply want to acquaint yourself with the countryside?'

'I've always been an inquisitive sort of chap,' he explained with a hint of embarrassment in his smile, 'and I prefer to explore things quietly on my own rather than in the company of a dozen or more students.'

'You're hoping to find something, then?' she questioned, and his smile deepened as he looked down into her amused face.

'A storm as violent as the one we have just had nearly always washes away the surface soil, and who knows what I might find.'

'The owner of the farm thinks you're wasting your time,' She proffered the information Lyle had given her.

'Perhaps we are,' Dennis agreed thoughtfully, 'but there's always the chance that the farmer might be wrong.'

'Are you always this optimistic?' she teased lightly, and his smile appeared again as he shook his dark head.

'I wouldn't say I'm optimistic,' he said, contradicting her description of him.

'Enthusiastic, then?' she corrected herself.

'That's nearer the mark,' he laughed, but his

expression sobered when he paused in his stride and turned to face her. 'The professor's a great archaeologist, and a wonderful lecturer. If I could be just a fraction as good as he is, I know I'll be satisfied.'

Christie hastily concealed the look of surprise that flashed across her face when she raised her glance to study Dennis thoughtfully. 'You admire him very much, don't you?'

'We all do,' came the quiet, sincere reply. 'He has a first-class knowledge of archaeology which leaves many of his colleagues lagging way behind, and yet we have never heard him crowing about his achievements. What we know about him is what we have read about him in the archaeological annals of recent years, and he has written some fabulous articles on the subject which we have found extremely helpful with our studies.'

Christie felt curiously shattered to discover how little she actually knew about the man she had once been married to. She had been too preoccupied with her own career and the sometimes unfair demands it made on her time to question Lyle about himself. She had known that he was an archaeologist of some repute, but he had never discussed his work with her, and there had never been time to enquire as to what it entailed, or what he had hoped to achieve.

A terrible sadness swamped Christie at the thought of what might have been, but this was not the time to dwell on past mistakes. Dennis was inspecting a deep *donga* caused by soil erosion over the years, and Christie stood about aimlessly while he leapt into the *donga* for a closer examination of something which had caught his eye.

'Hey, Christie, come and take a look at this!' His excited voice drew her swiftly back to the present. 'I think we have been excavating in the wrong place.'

The wet, spiky grass brushed against her legs when she walked towards the edge of the *donga* and stared down into it. A portion of the *donga* wall had caved in during the storm earlier that afternoon, and objects were jutting out of the remaining wall to reveal what looked like a treasure house of relics.

'That,' Dennis gestured expressively, 'will have to be removed with the utmost care, but look at this.'

He went down on his haunches and used his fingers to gently dig the mud away around an odd-looking object which projected from the reddish-brown soil at his feet.

'What is it?' she asked curiously.

'If I'm not mistaken, it's an iron spearhead,' Dennis enlightened her with growing excitement. 'Jump down and give me a hand.'

Christie did not need a second invitation. His excitement had fired her with a strange enthusiasm and, with a total disregard for her appearance, she slithered down into the *donga* and knelt down in the mud beside Dennis. Together, and very carefully, they dug the object out of the mud with their fingers until it lay in Dennis's hands. Christie sat back on her heels and was lost in thought while she observed Dennis. His face was aglow with satisfaction and pride, and a barely concealed excitement. Was this how Lyle had looked whenever he had found something of interest? Did his harsh features also soften with an expression of almost boyish delight?

They sat for some time studying what might have been an implement of war, or a weapon with which the warrior had hunted down food for his family, and Christie's curiosity finally got the better of her.

'How old would you say it is?'

'I would say it dates back a thousand years ... maybe less,' he shrugged. 'The professor will know for sure whether this is a relic from the Iron Age.'

He put the spearhead aside carefully, and continued digging gently in the area where he had found it, while Christie resumed her digging a little distance from him. She did not expect to find anything but, when her fingers eventually encountered something hard and smooth, she could not hide her excitement.

'Here's something else,' she said, her voice a whisper and her heart pounding while her fingers probed gently. 'It feels like an earthenware pot.'

'Be careful how you handle it,' Dennis warned hastily, leaving his own digging to kneel beside her. 'Whatever you do, don't force it out of the soil, or we might destroy something of archaeological value.'

'Don't you think I should ask Professor Venniker to join us here?' she questioned, leaving the digging to Dennis.

'Yes,' he nodded enthusiastically, 'and round up the rest of the team while you're in the camp.'

Christie climbed out of the *donga*, her sandalled feet slipping and her fingers digging deep into the mud to steady herself. She paused for a moment when she stood on the edge, and she smiled down at Dennis. 'This was your lucky day.'

'Only because you were here with me.'

'Thanks,' she laughed off his remark. 'I can feel myself shrinking to the size of a lucky charm.'

Her fine-boned features were devoid of humour, however, when she walked back to the camp. She did not want Dennis to develop a serious attachment to her. He had shown her kindness and consideration from the moment they had met, and she had been fortunate enough to share in his exciting discovery, but she knew that she could never offer him more than a casual friendship. She did not want to hurt him, and she could only hope that, if he was hovering on the edge of something more than friendship, he would have the good sense to know that there could be nothing else between them.

Lyle was still in his tent where she had left him almost an hour ago. The book was open on his lap, but he was leaning back in his chair with his eyes closed, and she marvelled, as she had always done, at the length and thickness of his black lashes.

'Lyle?' she murmured his name in a soft query, and his eyelids lifted at once. His critical glance shifted slowly down the length of her, and it was then that she became aware of what a frightful mess she must look. Her legs and hands were caked with mud, and her clothes were filthy. Embarrassment sent the colour flaring into her cheeks, and she wanted to turn and run from the mockery in his eyes, but the purpose of her mission gave her the courage to stay and face him. 'Dennis has found something in a *donga* beneath the digging site which he thinks you should take a look at, and perhaps the rest of the group could come as well,' she informed him in a breathless rush.

The mockery left his eyes at once. He snapped the book shut, put it aside, and rose to his feet in one lithe movement. 'Let's go,' he snapped.

The students were rounded up and, with Christie leading, they walked at a brisk pace up the hill towards the *donga*. A few bantering remarks were passed about Christie's dishevelled appearance, and some actually scoffed at the idea that Dennis may have found something of interest, but Lyle maintained a stony silence until they reached the *donga*, where Dennis had succeeded in prising the earthenware pot from the muddy soil.

A silence descended on the group as they gathered at the edge of the *donga*, but it was a silence laced with a quivering expectancy while Lyle's experienced glance took in the situation. Dennis looked up at him proudly, waiting as if for a signal from Lyle, and when it came the iron spearhead and the earthenware pot changed hands. Lyle studied the spearhead and passed it on to be circulated among the group, but he gave a great deal more attention to the earthenware pot which, unfortunately, had a sizeable piece missing out of its rim.

'It's Iron Age, wouldn't you say so, Professor?' Dennis spoke at last, breaking through the murmur of excited voices.

'It certainly appears to be, but we shan't know for certain until we have made an in-depth study of the strata.' Lyle frowned down at the pot in his hands, his fingers uncovering an engraved area beneath a layer of mud, then he glanced at Dennis and barked out an instruction. 'Mark the spot where you found these items, and leave that wall undisturbed. We'll cover this section of the *donga* with a canvas, and we'll move the equipment down here in the morning to start excavations in earnest.'

Christie stood a little aside from the group, and her glance was drawn irrevocably towards Lyle. His long-fingered hands were gently cradling the pot while he examined it, and there was a hint of a smile hovering about his stern mouth which gave Christie the impression that he was having difficulty in hiding his own enthusiasm. Dennis climbed out of the *donga* after carrying out Lyle's instructions, and Lyle's smile deepened when he glanced at the young man. 'Good work, Dennis.'

'It was Christie who found the earthenware pot, Professor,' Dennis enlightened him and, smiling broadly, he came to Christie's side and hugged her excitedly.

'Perhaps we'll make an archaeologist of her yet,' Lyle remarked cynically after a brief, electrifying pause while his glance rested on the arm that lingered about Christie's slender waist. He lost interest in her the next instant and directed his gaze at Dennis. 'Let's get back to the camp, then you can bring a couple of chaps up here to help you with the canvas.'

'Yes, sir,' Dennis grinned, allowing Christie to wriggle herself free of his arm.

What had begun as an excursion for practice and experience, had now become a bona fide excavation of relics which possibly dated back a thousand years, and if anyone had considered this trip a waste of time, then Dennis's discovery had put a buoyancy in their step. The excitement that rippled through the camp that afternoon was almost tangible, and it was contagious. Christie felt so much a part of it all that everything else was temporarily forgotten, and she was humming softly to herself when she went down the pool to wash herself. She bathed and changed into a clean pair of shorts and a shirt. She washed the things she had discarded, and she was still humming when she wrung out the excess water before wrapping her clothes in her towel.

Lyle was sitting in the office section of his tent when Christie approached it. Armed with a soft brush, he was removing the mud which clung to the earthenware pot, and there was intense concentration on his hawk-like features. Driven by curiosity, she stepped into the tent, and when she glanced at the pot over his shoulder she could almost understand why he found it so interesting that he appeared to be unaware of her presence. The engraving on the pot was not the usual, patterned design. It was engraved with an elephant holding its trunk aloft, and warriors were kneeling in its path with their faces pressed to the ground.

'That's an odd design.' Christie murmured her thoughts out loud without intending to, and Lyle looked up for the first time to acknowledge her presence with a cold, impersonal glance.

'I'm beginning to think that the legend of Indlovukazi has more reality attached to it than people have given it credit for.'

'What legend is this?' Christie questioned him, her glance still resting on the unusual design.

'Are you interested, or are you trying to be polite?'

'I'm interested,' she admitted, ignoring his sarcasm, and pulling up a chair to sit close to where Lyle was studying the relic she had discovered in the *donga*. 'Doesn't the name Indlovukazi have something to do with an elephant?' she asked, delving into her limited knowledge of one of the native languages.

'Directly translated it means "the great she elephant" and, quite likely, the legendary chieftainess was considered by her tribe to be as strong and fearless as an elephant, but Indlovukazi actually means "queen".'

'I'm relieved to hear that her size had nothing to do with her name.' Christie laughed at her own mental image of an enormous woman.

'Indlovukazi was reported to be a rather small woman.' His smile was faintly mocking when he put the pot aside and reached for his cigarettes. 'As you say, her size had nothing to do with the name she had been given.'

'Is it because of that unusual design that you suspect the legend of the tribal queen to be more than a legend?' she probed, her interest deepening.

'That, and several snippets of information I have picked up over the years,' he confessed, lighting a cigarette and blowing a cloud of smoke towards the ceiling of the tent. 'There's an old black man, Aaron, whose family lived on this land for centuries, and he believes that Indlovukazi's headquarters were situated in that cave above our digging site.' His expression hardened as he leaned back in his chair. 'This is all pure conjecture, of course, but if there is some truth in this story, then you have something in your possession which might once have belonged to that tribal queen.'

Christie felt a tremor of something close to shock racing through her, and her mind leapt around wildly before she recalled the small circular ivory disc which Lyle had given her shortly after their marriage. The design engraved around the outer edge of the flat disc had resembled intertwining branches, and in the centre had been the clear image of a man.

'Are you referring to that ivory disc you once gave me?' she queried hesitantly, her face paling to some extent when she recalled how little interest she had shown in his gift.

'That's correct,' came the abrupt reply. 'Aaron's great-grandfather had apparently found that disc in the cave, and it was eventually passed on to Aaron as the eldest son, along with the legend of Indlovukazi. The tribesmen of that time believed that their queen was someone god-like with powers beyond their imagination, and it was unheard of that such a woman should take a husband to suffer the emotions of ordinary mortals. They pampered her, doted on her and, when she had children, they firmly believed that she had obtained them through the process of her supernatural powers.'

'Of course, it wasn't like that at all.'

'Naturally not,' Lyle smiled cynically. 'Indlovukazi was human after all and, not wanting to act against her tribal customs, she took a lover and kept this knowledge hidden from her subjects. Indlovukazi and her lover are reputed to have been so besotted with each other that she commissioned a craftsman to make two small ivory discs, and they were to have been identically engraved except for the image in the centre. The one had to depict the image of a man, while the other had to depict that of a woman. Indlovukazi kept for herself the disc with the image of the man as a symbol of her lover and, as a symbol of herself, she gave her lover the disc with the image of a woman. They believed that, in this way, they would be together in spirit even when they had to be apart. Legend also has it that Indlovukazi had endowed these discs with certain powers so that they would be lovers for as long as those discs remained in their possession.'

'Did they always remain lovers?' Christie questioned him, a breathless catch in her voice as she found herself caught up in the dramatic events Lyle was relating to her.

'Unfortunately not,' Lyle spoke harshly, drawing hard on his cigarette and blowing the smoke in twin jets from his nostrils to lend a devilish appearance to his features. 'It was finally discovered that she had tricked her people, and her lover was put to death by the queen's infuriated followers.'

'And Indlovukazi?' Christie was holding her breath for some reason, her body taut with an inexplicable tension as she waited for the finale and, when it came, Lyle's deep, harsh voice injected a coldness into her veins.

'Stripped of the power she had wielded as the tribe's queen, and bereft of her lover, Indlovukazi committed suicide by stepping directly into the path of a rampant elephant.'

The image of a heartbroken Indlovukazi being trampled to death seemed to burn its way into Christie's soul, and she shuddered. 'Oh, how dreadful!'

'Perhaps not so dreadful if you believe that, in death, you will be free to join your lover.' Lyle's deep voice penetrated her disturbed thoughts.

'Perhaps not,' she agreed reluctantly, and it was some minutes before she could pull herself together sufficiently to ask, 'Why did Aaron give you the ivory disc?'

'Aaron doesn't have a son, and he knew that I was genuinely interested in the disc, as well as the legend attached to it.' Lyle's mouth twisted cynically. 'He also told me that it belonged with the woman I married.'

The woman I married. It was an unfortunate choice of words. It should have been *the woman I loved*, but it made her realise something she had ignored until that moment. Not once before, or during, their marriage had Lyle said that he loved her, and she wondered now whether *love* had ever featured in what he had felt for her.

'You never told me much about the disc when you gave it to me,' she accused, thrusting her painful thoughts into the recesses of her mind. 'You merely said that you believed it was one of a pair, and that you hoped one day to find the one which was missing.'

'As I recall, you weren't very interested five years ago,' he accused in turn, and she winced inwardly.

'That's not true, I——' She halted abruptly when a stab of guilt made her recall the occasion vividly. 'I admit that I was rather involved at that time,' she added lamely, lowering her eyes before the angry intensity of his glance.

'Involved with Sammy Peterson, yes, and a recording session for a new album,' he underlined her statement savagely.

'I'm sorry,' she heard herself apologising, her hands fluttering nervously before she laced her fingers together in her lap.

'I didn't ask for an apology, I was stating a fact.'

The desire to defend herself was an instinctive reaction, but she knew the futility of it a mere fraction of a second before the clanging of their improvised dinner gong interrupted their conversation.

Christie wrenched her glance from his, and picked up the wet bundle at her feet before she got up. She walked out of Lyle's tent with her head held high, but she could feel his accusing eyes boring into her back and, when she stepped into her tent, she had to clamp down hastily on the ridiculous desire to burst into tears. Lyle had spoken the truth. She had shown little interest in his gift, and her involvement in her career was no longer sufficient excuse for her negligence. The ivory disc lay at the bottom of her jewellery box, forgotten and overlooked for more than five years. Only now did she discover its significance: it was a symbol of love, but on its own it meant nothing, just as she meant nothing to Lyle.

CHAPTER FOUR

DURING their second week, and under Lyle's expert guidance, the archaeological students uncovered several items of interest. One item in particular caused a stir of excitement among the group. It was a string of roughly hewn gold beads. It lay embedded in the hard crust of the earth as it must have fallen a thousand years ago, but the leather thong which had once held them together had disintegrated with age. Wax was melted and poured into a shallow pan as a temporary mould, and the solid gold beads, when they were removed from the soil, were lain in the hardening wax in the exact formation in which they had been found.

Could it once have belonged to Indlovukazi? Christie's mind ran riot at the thought, and her growing interest in archaeology was like a flame leaping higher and higher inside her. Without Lyle's permission, or his approval, Christie involved herself physically with the excavations during the mornings, but her afternoons were spent taking down dictation and typing Lyle's notes while he discussed the day's findings with the students.

Their second week in the camp had been spent in much the same way as the first. On the Saturday morning Lyle took the Jeep and drove in to Dialsdrif with one of the students to collect fresh provisions for the week ahead, but the rest of the weekend was spent washing their clothes in the river, or simply relaxing after a hectic week.

On the Sunday morning an elderly black man strolled into the camp, and he spoke to Lyle for some time. It was after his departure that Christie discovered it had been Aaron, the man who had given Lyle the ivory disc which she had in her possession. Aaron had seen a snake near their camp, but it had disappeared into the bushes before he could kill it, and he had thought it best to warn them.

It was a blistering day, but Christie shivered at the thought of a snake lurking in the vicinity. The men searched through every tent, but found nothing, and it was generally assumed that the snake would shy away from entering the camp. Snakes were, after all, not in the habit of seeking out humans. It was a consoling thought, and the subject was not mentioned again.

Christie had, in fact, forgotten about it when she collapsed on the stretcher in her tent after lunch that Sunday. She felt exhausted and drained of her vitality in the heat, and she had barely closed her eyes when she drifted into a deep and dreamless sleep.

She must have slept for hours. It was dusk, and considerably cooler when she awoke with the sensation that her skin was crawling. Curious, yet reluctant to wake up, she lifted her lashes a fraction to see Lyle standing inside the flap of her tent. She thought at first that she was dreaming, but his face was strangely white, and she felt a very real stab of alarm. What was he doing in her tent? Her muscles tensed as she prepared to leap to her feet, but something made her lower her gaze, and what she saw was enough to chill the blood in her veins.

'Don't move!' Lyle's deep voice commanded

softly, but with an underlying severity. 'For God's sake, don't even move a muscle!'

Christie could not have moved at that moment even if she had been paid to do so. Stark fear had injected a numbness into her body that held her motionless on the stretcher while her terrified eyes were fixed on the reptile slithering across her legs, and up towards her right thigh. It's colour was grey, its length interminable, and its cold, slithery body was in no apparent haste to get wherever it wanted to be.

'In heaven's name, Lyle, *do* something!' she begged urgently through her clenched teeth.

'If I attempt to distract its attention it might just become infuriated, and it could turn on you,' he explained *sotto voce*, dashing her frantic desire for a quick escape. 'It's a black mamba, and it's dangerous.'

That last bit of information was of no comfort to her at all, and her heart was drumming out a violent tattoo of fear which brought her close to fainting. Oh, God, if only I *could* faint! she thought helplessly. Her face was white, and beads of perspiration were breaking out on her forehead like miniature pearls. Instead of fainting, she remained conscious and incapable of tearing her terror-stricken glance away from that forked tongue which darted repeatedly from the mamba's mouth as if he were licking his lips with relish at her discomfort.

It was moving up against her side, and she could no longer bear the feel of that cold, shifting body moving across her bare thighs. She wished now that she had worn slacks rather than shorts, and she suppressed a shudder of revulsion just in time. Lyle had warned her not to move, but if the mamba came near her face she knew that she would scream first, and contemplate the disastrous results afterwards.

Lyle was talking to her, his voice a low murmur of encouragement. She could not hear what he was saying, but it gave her the strength to lie there motionless while every other instinct cried out for her to brush that horrible reptile away from her. Every agonising second seemed like an eternity, and Christie could almost feel herself ageing when the snake raised its head close to her face. Her insides were shaking uncontrollably, and she was positive the mamba had picked up the vibrations emanating from her when she saw its head swaying back and forth while that forked tongue darted agitatedly from its mouth.

'You're doing fine,' Lyle encouraged, his voice finally penetrating that barrier of terror in her mind. 'It won't be much longer now.'

If one's supply of strength could be measured in quantity, then Christie was scraping together the dregs to survive the remaining seconds of this ordeal. That viperous head was lowered slowly, and that cold, slithery body brushed against her bare arm which was still raised on the pillow as she had slept. She closed her eyes momentarily, not sure how much she could bear, and then, miraculously, it was all over. The mamba's long body dropped to the floor, and Lyle moved in that instant with the speed of lightning. The downward thrust of a long-handled spade almost severed the viper's head from the rest of its wriggling body.

Christie found herself standing in the farthest corner of her tent. She had no recollection of how she had got there, but she was aware that she was shaking all over as Lyle lifted the reptile by the tail end of its body. It was almost as long as Lyle was tall, and a succession of shudders shook through her when he strode past her to fling it out of her tent. He turned, and his eyes were like dark pools in his white face as he stared at her. Christie was not conscious of moving, but she was in his arms the next instant, clinging to him a little wildly with her fingers digging into his muscled back, and her face buried against his broad chest. Lyle held her in silence until the tremors in her body subsided, and he continued to hold her when the silent tears of relief finally spilled on to her pale cheeks.

His hands worked their way through her hair, his touch comforting and soothing after the nightmare she had lived through, and she relaxed against the hard length of his body. There was comfort, too, in the familiar, woody scent of his masculine cologne, and she pressed closer to him as the horror of what might have happened shuddered through her. Her hands moved unconsciously across his back in a desperate need for reassurance rather than a caress, but she realised what she had done when she felt his body stiffen against hers.

'Damn you, Christie!' he muttered thickly, forcing her face out into the open, and her defences were down when he set his hard mouth on hers.

Her lips parted beneath the pressure of his, and he invaded her mouth with a mixture of anger and passion that seared her like a flame. She knew that she ought to push him away from her, but she felt too weak to do more than cling to him for support while her world dipped and swayed crazily about her. Her shattered mind was suddenly split in two. The one half issued a warning, while the other half preferred his angry passion to the savage hatred with which he had kissed her before.

She was released with an abruptness that brought an involuntary protest to her lips, but she knew the reason for it when she heard raised voices outside her tent.

Dennis and Alan stepped inside a second later with Erica and Valerie hovering directly outside. Christie stood like someone drugged while four pairs of eyes surveyed Lyle and herself with a mixture of expressions. She was vaguely aware that Lyle had regained his calm, unruffled appearance, and she could almost hate him for it when she was convinced that the evidence of his kisses were clearly visible on her tingling lips.

'Is that the snake Aaron was talking about this morning?' Dennis shattered the awkward silence, and he jabbed his thumb characteristically over his shoulder.

'I sincerely hope it is,' Lyle answered with some gravity. 'I suggest that we continue to exercise caution until we're sure this mamba didn't have a travelling companion.'

'Where did you find this monster?' the girls wanted to know, and their query was followed by a little shriek when Alan held the reptile up for the inspection of several other students who had gathered around the entrance to Christie's tent.

Christie shuddered at the sight of that long, grey body, and her reaction did not escape Lyle's notice. 'I found it in Miss Olson's tent,' he said abruptly and without elaborating the horrifying circumstances. 'Please dispose of it, Alan. I think Miss Olson has had her fill of snakes for one day.'

Lyle lingered a moment to see that Alan carried

out his instructions, then he strode out of Christie's tent, and left her feeling oddly bereft.

'Are you all right?' Dennis asked with concern, sliding a protective arm about Christie's shoulders. 'You're very pale, and you're trembling.'

'I—I'm fine,' she lied, her mind cruelly giving her a visual replay of what had occurred, but she pulled herself together hurriedly when her skin began to crawl with the memory of that reptile sliding over her. 'What I need most at this moment is a bath.'

'We're coming with you,' Erica and Valerie said almost in unison, and Dennis wandered off a little dejectedly while they collected their towels and hurried down to the pool before the darkness of night made it unsafe for them to bathe.

Christie was relieved to know that she had company, and relieved also to have a valid excuse to get away from her tent. The mere thought of having to return to it sent shivers up her spine, and she felt certain that she would never spend another peaceful night on that stretcher after what she had endured. The girls seemed to sense her reluctance to be alone, and they remained with her in her tent while she changed into fresh slacks and a cool sweater. Their conversation was light, their laughter almost gay, and Christie was terribly grateful to them for attempting to take her mind off what had occurred.

That night, when they sat around the open fire singing to Alan's guitar strumming, Christie lingered longer than usual. She was afraid to walk unescorted into her darkened tent. What if there was another snake, and what if Lyle was too late this time to help her? She shuddered at the thought, and she was tempted to ask someone to accompany her, but she could not bear the thought of Lyle's mockery.

The group around the fire diminished gradually, and Christie knew that she would make her nervousness obvious if she continued to sit there until everyone had gone. She got up at length, said good night, and literally forced her unwilling legs to carry her in the direction of her tent. Her skin crawled, and uncontrollable shivers raced up and down her spine when she pushed the flap aside and stepped into the tent. Her teeth were clenched so tightly together that her jaw ached, and she could feel the perspiration breaking out on her forehead when she fumbled for the box of matches. Her fingers were shaking so much that she had difficulty in lighting the candle, and when it was burning she cast a swift, nervous glance around the interior of the tent. There were too many shadows, and too many dark corners which she could not see into, but she undressed herself quickly and almost leapt on to her stretcher for fear that something might be lurking in the shadows beneath it.

She doused the flame of the candle, but she knew that she would not sleep. She sat curled up on the stretcher until the singing had stopped and everyone had gone to bed, but even then she knew that sleep would continue to evade her. She found herself listening intently for any little sound which might indicate that she was not alone, and her body was so tense that her muscles began to ache in protest.

Christie had no idea how much time had elapsed while she sat there trying to summon up sufficient courage to close her eyes and go to sleep. She struck a match to look at the time. More than an hour had passed; an hour of straining her ears for the sound of a possible intruder, and she shivered again at the memory of what might have happened if Lyle had not been there to help her through that ordeal.

'This is ridiculous!' she muttered to herself angrily.

She pulled her slacks and sweater on over her skimpy pyjamas, and swung her feet to the ground to push them into her sandals. The incident that afternoon had been something quite out of the ordinary, she told herself. It was quite likely that the snake had innocently sought refuge in her tent, but that did not eliminate the horrifying fact that *she* had been in the tent at the time.

An involuntary shiver ran up Christie's spine. She had to be sensible about this, and a breath of fresh air might help her come to her senses. She pushed aside the tent flap and stepped outside, her wary glance carefully avoiding the spot where the snake had lain after Lyle had flung it out of her tent, and she drew the cool night air slowly and deeply into her lungs to steady herself.

The moon was full in the star-studded sky, and the earth was bathed in a silvery glow that made it possible for her to see every blade of grass, and every motionless leaf on the trees. Something stirred to her right, and her heart skipped a nervous beat. She turned her head sharply in that direction, and saw Lyle standing at the entrance to his darkened tent. He was smoking a cigarette, and he was gazing so intently in her direction that her natural instinct was to dash back into her own tent, but she forced herself to remain where she was.

Christie stared back at him in silence. She had

not intended to seek out his company, but she was suddenly desperate for his comforting presence. She wanted to walk up to him, but she remained hesitant, and after seemingly endless seconds it was Lyle who made the first move. He dropped his cigarette, and crushed it beneath the heel of his shoe before he sauntered towards her.

'Can't you sleep?' he asked when he stood no more than a pace away from her.

'No, I can't,' she laughed shakily. 'I know it's silly of me, but I get the shivers at the mere thought of shutting my eyes and going to sleep in that tent.'

'It's a natural reaction.'

His reply, devoid of mockery and derision, stunned her momentarily into silence. She had not expected such calm understanding from Lyle, and she found herself relaxing slowly.

'I haven't thanked you yet for what you did this afternoon.'

'Forget it,' he said abruptly, his fingers latching on to her arm. 'What we both need is a stiff drink.'

He was ushering her towards his tent, and somehow she was incapable of protesting. He drew up a chair for her, and she sat with her hands locked together nervously in her lap until Lyle had lit a candle. He produced a bottle and two glasses from somewhere, and poured a shot of amber liquid into each glass while Christie observed him surreptitiously. His shirt was unbuttoned, and he had pulled it out of the confining belt which hugged his grey slacks to his lean hips. His dark hair lay across his forehead as if his fingers had paved their way through it incessantly, and she felt guilty when she sensed his annoyance and agitation.

'I'm sorry, Lyle. I never intended to make a nuisance of myself.'

He turned abruptly, glass in hand, and an unfathomable expression in his eyes. 'Drink this.'

'What is it?' she asked cautiously, carefully avoiding the touch of his fingers when she took the glass from him.

'Brandy,' came the clipped reply.

'I don't——'

'Drink it and shut up!' he interrupted harshly, and something in the set of his hard jaw told her that it would be wiser to choose the path of least resistance.

Christie raised the glass to her lips. The smell was enough to make her wrinkle her nose in distaste, but the first mouthful had her choking and gasping for breath until tears streamed down her cheeks. The inside of the tent dipped and wheeled as she brushed away the tears with the back of her hand and, when she finally got her breath back, she gasped, 'It tastes revolting!'

'You're to drink every drop,' Lyle instructed, swallowing down a mouthful of his own drink. 'It will settle your nerves.'

'It will make me tipsy,' she protested as the interior of his tent began to right itself around her.

'If it does make you tipsy, then you may consider it part of the adventure you were looking for when you applied for this job,' he mocked her.

'You're being nasty again,' she pointed out, that burning warmth inside her building up a confidence which bordered on boldness.

'Didn't you say you wanted to do something different—something adventurous?' he demanded, the mockery in his eyes deepening as he observed her heightened colour in the candle-light.

'Yes . . . sort of,' she admitted reluctantly, 'but that didn't include a frightening encounter with a snake, and getting drunk in the middle of the night.'

'It's the unexpected that makes life an adventure.' His mouth curved in a cynical smile. 'Didn't you know that?'

'I'm learning,' she answered drily.

His glance was lowered to the glass in her hand and it rose again to meet hers. It was a silent command to finish her drink, and she raised the glass to her lips. The second mouthful was not as lethal as the first, and the remainder was almost bearable. A stab of fiery warmth hit her stomach, and from there it spread into her limbs to make them feel curiously limp while her brain felt as if it was being stuffed with cotton wool. She was beginning to feel dizzy and light-headed, and totally unlike herself when she leaned forward to place the empty glass on the table.

'More brandy?'

'No, thanks,' she declined hurriedly. 'I think my nerves have been shuffled back into their proper order, but I wish I could say the same about my head.'

'You never did have a head for alcohol,' he reminded her, draining his own glass.

'You're right,' she laughed, her brain still clear enough to register the fact that the pitch of her low, musical voice was a semi-tone higher than usual. 'One glass of champagne is usually enough to give me the giggles.'

'I know.'

Those two words were sufficient to flood her mind with memories she would have preferred to forget. She was reminded of her wedding day, and her nervousness despite the fact that she had been very much in love with Lyle. That night, in their hotel room, he had ordered a bottle of champagne and, after one glass, she had erupted into a fit of giggles which he had found amusing rather than annoying. The giggles had eventually subsided, but it had also stripped her of her inhibitions, and she had followed rapturously where Lyle had led during that night of love.

Hot and embarrassed by the intimate trend of her thoughts, she rose abruptly to her feet, but that was a mistake. Her action had brought her so close to Lyle that her senses were at once tormented by the faint odour of his masculine cologne. The alcohol had helped to lower her guard, but she still had the sense to know that she had to leave before she made a complete fool of herself.

'I think I should——'

'Why did you cut your hair?' His quietly spoken query cut into her polite attempt to excuse herself from his now disturbing presence.

'The long hair was part of the image Sammy had wanted me to project,' she heard herself answering him. 'When my contract expired I shed the image along with my hair.' His maleness was still as potent as a drug, and she knew that if she was to escape unscathed she would have to get away from him quickly. 'Thanks for the drink, I think I'll sleep now.'

Christie moved away from him, almost stumbling over the chair in the process, but Lyle was beside her in an instant. 'I'll walk with you to your tent.'

'That won't be necessary,' she protested, her nerve ends quivering in mad response to his nearness. 'There's a full moon, and I can see quite clearly in the dark.'

She willed her legs to carry her away from him, but his arm was hard and warm about her waist before she had succeeded in taking the first step.

'You're trembling.'

That did not surprise her in the least. Her entire body had begun to pulsate with an awareness of danger, and she stammered foolishly, 'I—I can't imagine w-why.'

'Can't you?' His fingers were beneath her chin, tipping up her face, and the smouldering fire in his eyes made the blood pound faster through her veins. 'I think we have both known that something like this might happen. It was unavoidable, and there is no sense in fighting against it.'

She wished she could have said that she did not know what he was talking about, but that would not have been true. If nothing else remained, then the physical attraction was still there, and it was as strong now as it had been five years ago. For Christie the attraction went far deeper. She had fought against it, she had denied it, but now she could no longer ignore it. She still loved this man who had walked out on their marriage all those years ago.

His arm about her waist tightened, and she was caught up against his hard body. She could see the danger signals flashing in those compelling eyes, and she could feel it in the fingers sliding in a lazy caress along her cheek. Her lethargic mind came alive and flashed out a desperate warning, but her body refused to listen. She stood there in the circle of his arm, almost too afraid to breathe, her heart pounding against his hand which was spread out across her rib-cage.

Christie felt oddly weightless as Lyle muttered something unintelligible and turned her fully into his embrace. Her hands were against his hair-roughened chest in a half-hearted attempt to ward off the inevitable, but the texture and warmth of his skin against her palms ignited a flame inside her. She could feel his heart beating as wildly as her own, and she had a brief glimpse of a faintly triumphant gleam in his eyes before he snuffed out the flame of the candle.

She felt trapped in the moonlit darkness, chained by his arms, and drugged by the sensual, probing pressure of his mouth against hers. If she wanted to escape, then she had to do so now, but his hands were on her hips, moulding her body into the curve of his until the length of his thighs were pressed against her own. His hips moved against her, making her aware of his need, and a half-forgotten, quivering warmth erupted in the lower half of her body. If her mind was still urging her to resist, then she was no longer listening. Her emotions had taken over to dictate her actions, and her lips moved in response beneath his, while her hands slid up over his chest to become locked in the short dark hair at the nape of his neck.

Lyle drew back slightly, and for one terrible moment she thought that he had decided to reject her, but she was lifted in his arms as if she weighed nothing at all while he carried her into the area partitioned off as his sleeping quarters. His mouth sought hers again in the darkness when he set her on her feet, and her arms were still locked about his neck when his hands slid up beneath her sweater to cup the soft swell of her breasts.

'Lyle!' she groaned against his mouth, the familiar intimacy of his touch sending a breath of sanity wafting through her mind. 'This is ... crazy!' she protested weakly.

'I want you, and I'm damned if I'm not going to have you.'

'You'll hate yourself in the morning,' she warned, recalling against her will his displeasure, and his savage anger which she still failed to understand.

'I probably will hate myself,' he grunted, his lips against that fluttering pulse at the base of her throat. 'But at this moment I don't really care.'

'Oh, God!' she breathed jerkily when he lifted her sweater and pulled it off over her head.

The zip of her slacks offered no resistance, and he peeled off the rest of her clothes, lowering her on to the inflated mattress as he did so. Her sandals were tugged off and flung aside, and then he was shedding his own clothes before he followed her down on to the mattress.

He drew her closer to him with a hint of impatience in his touch, and he cradled her softness against his hard frame. His heated flesh against her own made her tremble with the awakening of long-suppressed emotions, and she felt strangely like someone who had arrived home after a long, tiresome journey. She combed her fingers through his hair for the sheer joy of feeling its softness, and drew his head down to hers until his mouth closed over her seeking, parted lips.

Lyle's hands explored her body, his fingers trailing over her heated skin like butterfly wings until it felt as if every nerve was vitally alive and tingling in response. His mouth left hers, and she drew a ragged breath as he trailed a path of burning kisses along her sensitive skin, across her creamy shoulder and down to her breasts. With his lips and tongue he teased the rosy peaks of her breasts into hard buttons of achingly sweet desire, and it was then, for one fleeting moment, that an element of doubt entered her drugged mind once again. This was wrong. They were bound to regret their actions. Withdrawal was the answer, but Lyle's hand slid down across her flat stomach, and the intimacy of his caress left no room for coherent thought. The fire inside her was being coaxed into a raging inferno, and her taut, quivering body was aching for the fulfilment it had been denied all these years.

'Lyle...' Her voice was a husky whisper, and almost unrecognisable as her desire mounted with every intimate caress. 'It's been ... so long.'

'Do you want me?' he questioned throatily and, intoxicated with the sensations he was arousing, she could not lie to him.

'You know I do.'

'Say it so that I can know you mean it,' he commanded.

'I want you,' she obeyed him like someone without a mind of her own while she planted frantic little kisses along his throat and shoulder, tasting the damp saltiness of his skin against her tongue. 'I want you.'

'How many men have there been these past five years?'

'There haven't ... been any ... men,' she gasped, his lips and hands on her burning flesh arousing her to a fever pitch of desire she had never known before.

'Do you expect me to believe that?' he continued to interrogate her while her conscious mind was in no position to object.

'God help me, it's ... the truth!'

His hands stilled on her body, and his eyes glittered strangely in the semi-darkness when he raised his head. 'I think I actually believe you.'

'Lyle, *please*!' she begged hoarsely, her hands clutching at his wide shoulders, and her taut body aching with a need which was becoming almost intolerable. 'Don't torment me like this!'

Her plea seemed to amuse him. He laughed throatily, but it was a triumphant laugh tinged with an anger she did not have time to analyse. His desire unleashed was something violent, and in the fusion of their bodies Christie smothered a cry of protest and pleasure against Lyle's shoulder.

She was conscious only of the feel and taste of him as the thrusting rhythm of his body piled sensation upon sensation until that exquisite tension snapped inside her, and spiralled repeatedly throughout her entire body.

Christie felt the shuddering weight of Lyle's body pressing her deeper into the mattress, and his groan of pleasure added to her joyous satisfaction. His heart was thundering into hers with a force and swiftness that matched her own, and Christie could almost make herself believe that the nightmare of the past five years had been a figment of her imagination.

Lyle nuzzled that sensitive spot behind her ear and growled unsteadily, 'I'd forgotten how good it was to make love to you.'

He had forgotten how good it was to make love to her. Was that all he could say? Disappointment hastened the transition from rapture to reality and, when Lyle rolled away from her a few moments later, her mind was filled with cold logic rather than contentment.

'Were there many women, Lyle?'

'There were a few,' he admitted, sitting up with his broad back facing her while an icy, unreasonable anger surged through her. She got up and dressed herself without looking at Lyle, but she must have conveyed some of her displeasure to him during those awkward, silent moments. 'I'm a man, Christie, and I have a normal sexual appetite,' he announced with an angry impatience. 'Did you imagine I would live the life of a celibate after our marriage collapsed?'

Christie could not answer that question, but she retaliated swiftly with a question of her own. 'Is Sonia Deacon one of those women?'

She was observing him over her shoulder while she zipped herself into her slacks, and she was grateful for the darkness in the tent when his cold, controlled voice rebuked her with, 'That's none of your business!'

He could not have hurt her more if he had plunged a knife into her heart. Fiery tears stung her eyes, but somehow she managed to hold her head high when she walked out of Lyle's tent. She despised him, but at that precise moment she despised herself a great deal more.

CHAPTER FIVE

CHRISTIE awoke on the Monday morning with a feeling of dread lodged like a heavy weight on her chest. She could not at first think why, and then she remembered every intimate and embarrassing detail of what had happened between Lyle and herself in the night. She had been a fool to allow herself to be ruled by her emotions, and now she would have to pay the price for her folly. She felt cheap and small, and she had no idea how she was going to cope with having to face Lyle during the remaining two weeks of their stay in the bushveld.

The students were moving about in the camp, and the hiss of the gas stove told her that breakfast was being prepared. Christie wriggled out of her sleeping bag and poured water into the plastic basin on the stand in the corner of the tent. She washed and brushed her teeth, wishing that she could wash away that feeling of cheapness, but it lingered like an invisible label to remind her of her foolishness. She cursed Lyle silently, but she cursed herself even more for allowing herself to be caught up in that trap of emotion she had practically set up for herself. The motivation for her had been *love*, but for Lyle she had simply been one of the many women he had made love to over the years. *I'd forgotten how good it was to make love to you*, he had said. Perhaps she should have taken that as a compliment, but instead she had been left with the feeling that she had behaved like a cheap wanton who had been only too willing to add her name once again to that long list of his conquests.

She groaned inwardly, realising that the only good thing about last night was that it had helped her to forget about the mamba and her nervousness of being alone in her tent.

The saucepan clanged to announce that breakfast was ready, and she steeled herself to go out and face Lyle. He was standing with his back to her, talking to Dennis and Mike while they waited to be served, and Christie's unobtrusive glance took in the width of his shoulders beneath the blue shirt, and the khaki shorts hugging his lean hips. His long, muscular legs were tanned, and his feet were encased in comfortable suede boots. She could still recall the feel of his lean, hard body against her own, and a hot flush stained her cheeks when she thought of the intimacies they had shared. He looked up when she passed him, and his cool, impersonal glance was like a reviving shot in the arm when she took her place at the end of the queue and tried to ease the rapid beat of her heart.

'Take it easy! Stay calm!' she warned herself, but, when she recalled how Lyle had questioned her about her personal life, a stormy anger took possession of her. Crazed with passion, she had told him everything he had wanted to know, and he could no longer doubt that he was still the first and *only* man ever to touch her intimately. She had boosted his ego for him, and then he had literally slammed the door in her face by telling her to mind her own business where his sexual encounters were concerned.

Fury, like an angry volcano, simmered inside her. If Lyle had wanted revenge, then he had succeeded in his objective, but she would never forgive him for making her feel like a cheap slut who had been only too willing and eager to fall into bed with him.

It was Christie's anger that helped her through the rest of that gruelling day in the heat and dust. With a brush and a small trowel she worked alongside the students in their search for further evidence of a race which had existed a thousand years ago. The worst ordeal was having to sit down in Lyle's tent while he dictated the technical data pertaining to their findings that day. Her mind wandered back to the night before, cruelly conjuring up images of what had occurred, and it took a tremendous effort to sit there calmly, taking down what Lyle dictated while he paced about restlessly. Several times that morning she had caught him looking at her strangely, and he was looking at her now. She could feel his dark eyes boring into her, willing her to meet his probing glance, but she kept her eyes on her notebook with a determined effort that left her feeling drained and exhausted when she was finally left alone to get on with her typing.

Christie's head felt as if it had taken a battering that left it sensitive and bruised, and the shrill sound of the cicadas on that hot day aggravated the dull headache she had been nursing since early that morning. The heat was oppressive, as if a storm was brewing, but there were no clouds in the sky, and not the slightest suggestion of a breeze to ease her discomfort. She was drenched in perspiration when she pulled the last sheet of paper out of the typewriter. She longed for a refreshing swim in the river, and she was in no mood for a confrontation with Lyle when he walked into the tent and deliberately barred her way when she was about to leave.

'Where are you going?' he demanded, looking down at her from his great height with those strangely probing eyes.

'I have typed out your notes, and I was going down to the pool for a swim,' she explained tritely. 'Was there something else you wanted me to do, Professor?'

'Don't call me that!' he barked angrily.

'That's what you are, isn't it?'

'Dammit, Christie!' he exploded savagely in the wake of her sarcastic query, then he made a visible effort to control himself. 'About last night . . .'

'I don't wish to discuss it!' she interrupted him sharply, her hands clenched so tightly at her sides that her nails bit into her palms. 'It was something that should never have happened, and for the rest of my life I shall regret my part in it.'

An angry little muscle jerked along the side of his jaw. '*You* may regret it, but *I* don't.'

'I didn't think you would,' she retorted angrily, her blue eyes dark and stormy. 'You've had your revenge, and now I hope you will be satisfied.'

'What happened last night wasn't an act of revenge.'

'What was it, then?' she blazed up at him. 'An ego trip?'

'What the hell are you talking about?' he demanded harshly, taking her by the shoulder and spinning her round to face him when she attempted to make a timely exit.

'Apart from everything else, you asked a lot of questions last night, and you got a lot of straight answers,' she conceded furiously and sarcastically. 'Your ego must be so inflated at this moment that

I'm surprised you're still capable of walking with your feet on the ground.'

His mouth tightened with annoyance. 'In the name of all that's holy, Christie, will you calm down and let us discuss this situation sensibly and rationally?'

His hands reached for her, but she stepped back to put a comfortable distance between them. 'I have no desire to discuss the matter with you. Not now, or at any other time in the future.'

His expression was shuttered and his eyes had become narrowed slits of fury. 'I take it, then, that last night was no more than a brief, and perhaps pleasant interlude to you?'

'You may take it whichever way you please,' she brushed aside his query, hiding her pain behind a careless exterior.

'I would have preferred to think that last night meant something more to you, but it appears I was a fool to think so.'

Her eyes filled with scorching tears, but she had turned her back on Lyle, and she was relieved that he did not witness the effect of his stinging remark. She walked away from him before she made an even bigger fool of herself by believing that she might have been wrong in her assumption that he had made love to her simply for the sake of revenge. She had believed him once before. She had believed that he loved her even though he had never said so, and she had trusted him like a child, but he had walked out on her during the first crisis in their marriage.

Christie swallowed down a couple of aspirins in her tent. Her head was pounding as if someone was striking her with a sledge-hammer while she walked down to the Mogalakwena River with her towel draped over one rigid shoulder, and with every step it felt as if a knife was being thrust deep into her temples. She stripped at the water's edge and literally fell into the pool, deliberately wetting her hair, and the coolness of the water against her face and her scalp gradually eased her pulsating headache.

She felt exhausted when she got out of the water and dressed herself, but her headache had fortunately ceased. She sat on the rocks for some time, staring into space and quite oblivious of the beautiful crimson fingers stretching across the sky as the sun dipped in the west. She did not want to think or feel, but she could not find the peace she craved while Lyle's voice echoed in her mind.

I would have preferred to think that last night meant something more to you, but it appears I was a fool to think so.

What did it mean? What had he been trying to say? Oh, God, if only she could know!

If Christie had feared that Lyle might confront her again with the intention of discussing their relationship, then she was mistaken. He now spoke to her only when it was absolutely necessary, and at other times he ignored her completely. She ought to have been pleased, but instead she felt hurt and unhappy. It was at this point that she began to value the friendship Dennis had offered her from the start. His presence, at times, eased the awkward tension which had risen between Lyle and herself, and he could make her laugh even when she thought there was no more laughter left inside her.

The excavations seemed to be spiced with a new urgency, and there was little time for Christie to think about herself as she listed and numbered each item they found. Taking an active part in the excavations, and the excitement of perhaps finding a relic, made the days pass with an incredible swiftness.

'I have an idea the professor has been looking for something,' Dennis announced one evening towards the end of their stay, when they were sitting a little distance from the rest of the group around the fire, and Christie glanced at her companion with interest.

'What makes you think that?'

'It's just a feeling,' Dennis shrugged. 'He hasn't perhaps said anything to you, has he?'

'Not a word,' she assured him, her glance darting briefly to where Lyle sat smoking a cigarette with his back propped against the stem of a syringa tree. 'My relationship with Professor Venniker doesn't exactly include the exchange of confidences,' she added with a wry laugh.

'So I've noticed.'

His teasing remark veered towards the personal, and she hastily changed the conversation back to the subject they had been discussing. 'Do you have any idea what he could be looking for?'

'No,' Dennis frowned, 'but I think it's something with which he hopes to substantiate his theory that this territory once belonged to Indlovukazi, the legendary tribal queen.'

'I thought we had uncovered enough evidence these past weeks to substantiate his theory.'

'I thought so, too, but I have a feeling the professor won't be satisfied until he finds whatever it is he's looking for.' Dennis lowered his voice as he spoke, and he leaned towards Christie in a conspiratorial manner. 'Have you seen how the professor examines every fragment when the sifting is taking place?'

'I have noticed, yes,' she answered thoughtfully, taking his discussion seriously for the first time. 'What he's looking for must be small, I gather.'

'Or it could be fragments of something which was not so small in its original form,' Dennis added logically.

'Why don't you ask him what he's looking for?' she queried, wrapping her arms about her raised legs and resting her chin on her knees.

'I have asked him,' Dennis smiled ruefully, 'but it didn't really get me anywhere.'

'What did he say?'

'He laughed and told me I had an over-active imagination.'

Christie considered this for a moment, then a teasing smile lifted the corners of her mouth. 'Perhaps you have.'

Dennis flicked her arm with his finger in playful punishment, and their conversation ended there when Alan lifted his guitar on to his knee and strummed it softly.

Christie was pulled to her feet to join the group around the fire, and for one brief second her eyes met Lyle's, but that one look was sufficient to leave her feeling disturbed and chastened for the rest of the evening. Lyle had been furious, and his fury had been directed at her, but she could not imagine why.

A few days later Christie's brush and trowel uncovered a small jar in the wall of the *donga*. At other times she had left the removal of items in the skilled hands of the students, but on this occasion she felt an odd, driving need to do so on her own. She worked slowly, knowing that one careless move could break the jar, and it seemed to take agonising hours in the hot sun before the small jar came away from its resting place. Her hands were trembling with an excitement she could not understand, and when she turned the jar over between her fingers she heard the dull sound of objects rattling inside it. She tried to lift the lid, but nature had sealed it well to preserve its contents.

'You'll need a penknife and a brush to break the seal,' Dennis advised, running his finger lightly along the narrow slit between the lid and the rim of the jar.

Christie felt dubious about undertaking such a delicate task on her own, but at the same time she was almost jealous at the thought of someone else taking over. 'Do you think I could do it?'

'You found the jar,' Dennis smiled, lending her his own penknife. 'I would say the privilege to open it is yours.'

It sounded like a challenge; it *was* a challenge, and she climbed out of the *donga* with the small jar held protectively against her body. She darted a glance at Lyle, but he was involved in a discussion with a handful of students and, spreading a small sheet of canvas beneath a shady tree, Christie began the nerve-racking task of breaking the jar's seal without damaging it.

Once again she worked slowly, using the knife and the brush alternately. If she forced the lid of the clay jar it could be marred, so she took her time, even though her insides were quivering with a feverish haste. She felt again that strange excitement rippling through her. It tingled along her spine and spread along her arms into her fingertips, making her all the more determined to discover what was hidden in that small black jar.

It seemed to take an eternity of scraping and brushing to succeed in her objective. She worked the knife deeper and deeper into that groove between the lid and the mouth of the jar, and she was close to relinquishing her efforts when the lid moved a fraction. Christie's heart leapt into her throat, and her hand was shaking when she put down the knife and picked up the brush to dust away the soil she had loosened. To make sure that she had not imagined it, she slid the point of the knife once again in a circular motion around the lid, and she was rewarded by a crunching, gritty sound as the lid shifted its position.

Her heart was pounding aginst her ribs as she cast a searching glance around the digging site. It was almost time to return to the camp for lunch. The students were packing away their tools, and Lyle was still examining the tiny particles of clay and stone which had remained in the sieve. She would have to hurry, there was little time left. *Time for what?* she wondered absently, but she did not wait to find the answer. Using the sharp point of the knife, she carefully lifted off the lid, then she tilted the jar and emptied its contents out on to the small sheet of canvas.

For one dreadful moment it felt as if all the air had been squeezed out of Christie's lungs, and a strange iciness took possession of her as she stared at the objects spread out on the green sheet of canvas. Surrounded by four lion fangs and a small iron spearhead, was an ivory disc of about five centimetres in diameter, and it was an exact replica of the disc Christie had in her possession, except for the figure of a woman carved in the centre.

This was the disc which Indlovukazi had given to her lover as a token of her love, and *this*, Christie realised, was what Lyle had been searching for.

She fingered the disc almost reverently. It was yellowed with age, but it was beautifully preserved, and she felt again that tingling excitement racing through her when she picked it up at last and held it between her trembling fingers.

'It's time to go,' Lyle's voice rang out clearly and, acting on a crazy impulse, Christie slipped the disc into the pocket of her denim shorts.

She felt guilty, but no one had seen her, she was certain of that, and she hastily scraped together the remaining objects. She returned them to the jar and carefully replaced the lid before gathering up the rest of her things.

Lyle stood some distance from her, and he appeared to be frowning into the distance. He was obviously lost in thought, but the sound of her step behind him made him turn at once, and his glance seemed to be drawn like a magnet to the jar resting in the palm of her hand.

'Where did you find that?'

'In the *donga*,' she explained with a new kind of anxiety knotting her nerve ends. 'I've marked the spot and numbered it.'

He took the jar from her and examined it; when he looked up, his eyes were narrowed slits of anger. 'Who gave you permission to break the seal?'

'I did,' Dennis answered, coming up behind Christie. 'And I don't think any of us could have made a better job of it,' he added, glancing at the lid which was still in perfect condition.

Lyle's mouth tightened, but he left the matter

there, and directed his sharp gaze at Christie. 'Did you examine the contents?'

'Yes, I did,' she confessed, and Lyle gestured towards the sheet of canvas in her hands, indicating that she should spread it out on the ground.

'The owner of this jar appears to have been a sentimentalist,' Lyle observed drily when he studied the objects lying spread out on the canvas. 'I'm inclined to think he kept the fangs of the first lion he killed, and also the spearhead with which he accomplished it.' He sat back on his heels, turning the objects repeatedly between his fingers, then he looked up sharply and captured Christie's nervous gaze. 'Was this all you found in the jar?'

It felt as if the ivory disc was burning a hole in her pocket. Her rational mind told her to hand over what did not belong to her, but for some obscure reason she decided against it.

'That was all,' she lied.

Lyle's dark glance held hers, and she had a horrible feeling that guilt was written all over her hot face. She had never been a good liar, nor was it in her nature not to tell the truth, and she was subconsciously horrified at what she was doing.

'How odd,' Lyle broke the tense little silence. 'To my knowledge the people of a thousand years ago seldom placed anything in a jar with a lid unless they wished to conceal something, but I can't imagine why the owner of this jar would have wanted to conceal the evidence of his bravery.'

He knew! She was positive that he knew! She had time to rectify the matter, but still she hesitated.

'Perhaps he was a modest man,' Dennis suggested helpfully.

'Primitive man was never modest,' Lyle contradicted cynically. 'It was important to make his strength and bravery known if he wanted to be acknowledged as an adult male in the community.'

'In that case, Professor,' Dennis shrugged characteristically, 'the man must have been a sentimentalist as you suggested.'

'He must have been,' Lyle agreed with a faint smile as he gathered up the objects and rose to his full, imposing height. 'Let's get back to the camp.'

They did not speak on the way down. Christie went into her tent to wash her face and hands before lunch, and afterwards she dipped her fingers into the pocket of her shorts to reassure herself that the ivory disc was still there.

What on earth had possessed her to slip it into her pocket? And why had she remained silent about its existence?

Christie stood motionless, her fingers touching the disc in her pocket, and it was then that she knew the incredulous truth. Deep down inside she was nursing the impossible hope that fate would be kind, and that she would be given the opportunity to hand this disc to Lyle as a token of her love for him. Her legs felt weak, and her insides were shaking when she joined the others for lunch. It was idiotic to hope that she would ever be given such an opportunity, and it was crazy to think that she could re-enact Indlovukazi's actions of a thousand years ago. Lyle did not love her and, unless she was certain of his feelings, she would never let him know exactly how she felt about him. The two discs belonged together, and they belonged with two people who loved each other. Did she hope that the tribal queen's powers would somehow reach across the ages into the twentieth century, and that her possession of the two discs would bring Lyle back to her?

That was ridiculous! Her logical mind answered that query, but from the illogical recesses of her mind she knew that this was exactly what she did hope for. It was madness, but, loving him as much as she did, she was willing to cling to every fragile hope ... or belief.

She dipped her fingers into her pocket while she ate her lunch, and touched the ivory disc. She would have to think of a safe place to keep it, but at the moment there was no safer place than on her person.

The last two days were hectic and, when they gathered around the camp fire for the last time, their sadness at having to leave was evident in the melancholy words of the songs they chose. Alan fumbled for the chords on the guitar in his customary manner, and Christie saw a look of irritation flash across Lyle's lean face where he stood leaning against a tree with a cigarette dangling from his fingers. Their eyes met across the camp fire, and something in the way he looked at her sent a warning flashing through her mind, but she was still unprepared for what followed.

'I would like to make a suggestion,' Lyle addressed Alan. 'Lend your guitar to Christie, and let her sing for a change.'

Christie was startled by this unexpected exposure. She felt a numbness surging through her during the ensuing silence, and her nerves knotted at the pit of her stomach when fifteen pairs of eyes were suddenly focused on her. *Damn* Lyle for doing this to her! She assumed that he found a sadistic pleasure in revealing her secret, and hurt mingled with anger as she glared at him. She started to rise to escape all the attention, but the guitar was placed in her hands, and she sat down helplessly with the instrument cradled in her lap.

'I knew it!' Erica shattered the silence with her shrill, excited voice. 'I had a feeling you were the folk singer my brother was so crazy about, but the photographs on your albums never did you justice, and your short hair had me confused.'

'Stop chattering, Erica, and let Christie sing,' someone admonished her laughingly.

The group fell silent once again, and Christie stared down at the instrument in her hands with an uncommon nervousness. 'I really don't think I can——'

'Come on, Christie, it's our last night together,' Erica interrupted her vaguely formulated protest. 'Sing one of your favourite songs.'

Lyle's dark gaze issued a challenge which she could not ignore, and she responded with a challenge of her own. She chose a song which she had composed shortly after meeting Lyle. It was of special significance to both of them, and it had, at that time, summed up their feelings most aptly.

The silence was expectant when Christie's practised fingers coaxed the opening bars of the song from the guitar, and the tightening of Lyle's mouth told her that he had recognised it at once. The melody was haunting and, injecting a husky intimacy into her usually warm, vibrant voice, she sang:

> The first time we touched I knew
> There could never be anyone but you.
> Your eyes met mine

> And I had to believe
> This was not just a moment in time.
>
> I'd never known love before,
> But you promised all that, and more.
> I felt your touch,
> Your kiss was like wine,
> And I knew that this moment was mine.
>
> Near or far apart
> You will always have my heart.
> I spend the hours
> Hoping you will find
> It was not just a moment in time.

Christie knew that she had the complete, almost stunned attention of her small audience as she took the song through to its emotional end. There was a mesmerised silence when her voice faded dramatically on the last note, then the silence erupted with cries of, 'More! More!'

She was surprised to find that her eyes were misty with emotion, and when she searched for Lyle he was no longer there. Christie had no idea when he had left, but his absence told her, in no uncertain terms, that he no longer cared.

'One more, Christie! Just one more song!' her small audience pleaded, but Christie was too choked to speak, let alone sing.

'No!' Dennis stepped into the breach when he became aware of her distress and, taking the guitar from her, he handed it back to Alan. 'I think we'll end the evening on that beautiful note,' Dennis added. 'We have a long drive ahead of us tomorrow, and we all have to get up early.'

The group around the fire dispersed reluctantly, and Dennis accompanied Christie to her tent. Her glance searched the camp area for Lyle, but he was nowhere in sight, and that lump in her throat became an aching obstruction.

'That song,' Dennis began, breaking the silence between them when they paused at the entrance to her tent. 'You wrote it for someone special, didn't you?'

'Yes,' Christie forced the word past the lump in her throat while her eyes still probed the shadows for Lyle's familiar figure.

'Am I wrong in thinking that you wrote it for someone like the professor?'

Christie's body went rigid, and Dennis had her complete attention for the first time 'What are you trying to say?' she asked warily.

He had been studying her intently, but she sensed his sudden embarrassment when he looked away and kicked at an imaginary stone. 'I walked past the professor's tent that afternoon after we had discovered the relics in the *donga*,' he explained, 'and I heard him mention to you that he had given you something five years ago which you hadn't shown much interest in.'

The ivory disc. Her hand went automatically to the pocket of her slacks, but the carved disc was no longer there. She had hidden it away safely among her personal toiletries, and it would remain there until she could reunite it with its replica.

'So, now you know that Professor Venniker and I didn't meet each other for the first time on the university campus four weeks ago,' Christie remarked with forced casualness.

'But it's more than that, isn't it,' Dennis summed up the situation between Lyle and herself and, when she stood there speechless with surprise and indecision, he touched her arm lightly. 'I'm sorry, Christie, but when I discovered that you and the professor had known each other before, I couldn't help recalling how antagonistic you were towards each other from the start of this trip. Since then I've been watching you closely, and I've seen the way you look at him.'

'Dear heaven!' she groaned inwardly, wondering if her behaviour had been as transparent to everyone else.

'When you sang that song,' Dennis continued, 'and when I saw how the professor reacted, I knew that your relationship had been more than simply a casual acquaintance.'

'How did he react?' she could not help asking.

'He looked furious, as if someone had carelessly dropped a priceless relic, and just before the end of your song he stalked off in the direction of the river.' The crickets chirped lustily in the undergrowth when Dennis added persuasively, 'Care to tell me about it?'

Tiredness washed over her like a weighted blanket, and she sighed heavily. 'It's a long story, Dennis, and ... some other time, perhaps.'

'Does that mean you will let me see you when we're back in Johannesburg?'

'You've been a good friend these past weeks,' she replied, not wanting to commit herself, then she touched his cheek lightly with her fingers. 'Good night, Dennis.'

She left him there, and pushed aside the flap of her tent to go inside, but it was some hours before she eventually stopped tossing and went to sleep for the last time in her bushveld tent.

CHAPTER SIX

THE tents had been taken down, the equipment had been loaded on to the trucks, and the precious cargo packed firmly into the Microbus for a gentler ride back to the city. Nothing remained to indicate it had been a camping site, except for their footprints in the dust, and the dead ashes of the previous night's fire. Christie stared about her with a rising lump in her throat. Tomorrow this would all be a memory, but, like some memories, this was one which she knew she would never forget.

'You're coming with me,' Lyle barked at her when she would have got into the truck beside Dennis, and Christie was not in the mood to argue, or to question this unexpected decision of his.

She followed Lyle towards the Jeep parked in a spot which was shaded from the heat of the early morning sun. She dumped her bag on to the back seat, and Lyle was already seated impatiently behind the wheel when she got in beside him. He turned the key in the ignition the moment she slammed the door shut, and the roar of the Jeep's engine was the signal for the other vehicles to follow. Christie took one last look at the open patch among the trees, then she slumped back into her seat and sat there fighting against that aching tightness in her throat. She wanted to cry, but she was damned if she was going to do so in front of Lyle.

It was going to be another long, hot day, and

the trip back to Johannesburg was going to take hours. Lyle's blue shirt was open almost to his waist, and his grey trousers spanned tighly across his muscular thighs. His strong hands rested lightly on the steering wheel, and when she risked a quick glance at his face she found his profile stern and forbidding. It was sad, she thought, that one could be so close to someone, and yet so terribly far away. If only it could have been different.

'I'm sorry about last night,' she felt compelled to say the minute they jolted off the uneven track on to a smoother gravel road. 'It was in poor taste to choose a song which would remind you of a period in your life which you would much rather not dwell on.'

'Forget it!' he brushed aside her apology, his expression unaltered as he changed gear and put his foot down on the accelerator. 'The reason why I wanted you to travel with me this morning was because I want to talk to you about Dennis.'

'What about Dennis?' she asked, instantly on her guard.

'He still has several years of studying ahead of him.' A cynical smile twisted Lyle's mouth. 'He's also too young for you, and too inexperienced.'

'And what is that supposed to mean?' she demanded, barely managing to hang on to her temper.

'Leave him alone, Christie,' Lyle warned harshly. 'He's a brilliant scholar, and I don't want him distracted in any way, or hurt by someone like yourself.'

'Hold on a moment!' Blue sparks of angry fire darted from her eyes when she turned in her seat to face him. 'You're behaving as if I'm some sort of Delilah who is planning to seduce Dennis and destroy him.'

Lyle's hands tightened on the wheel. 'I'm sorry if I gave that impression, but he has the potential to become one of our country's leading archaeologists, and I don't want anything, or anyone, to spoil his chances.'

'I should imagine he's old enough to take care of himself,' she snapped, her voice pure acid. 'And why are you so concerned about him anyway?'

'He's the son of a fellow archaeologist who is a friend as well as someone I respect and admire very much.'

'And it might ruin a great friendship if it should become known that his son has become involved with your ex-wife?' she finished for him sarcastically.

'Dammit, Christie!' he exploded with a violence that made her shrink from him in the confined space of the Jeep. 'It's not that at all!'

'Then why do you make it seem as if I have committed a crime by being friendly with Dennis?'

Lyle cast a brief, angry glance in her direction. 'Dennis wants more than friendship from you, and if you don't know that already, then you have less sense than I gave you credit for.'

Christie felt her anger and indignation drain away from her. It was true. She *had* noticed Dennis's interest in her, and she *had* known that she would have to do something about it before it went too far, but it did not do her any good to have Lyle reminding her of something she had neglected to carry out.

'All right!' she snapped at length, gesturing expressively with her hands. 'I admit that I think he has a bit of a crush on me, but I know it will pass, and I don't want to hurt him with an outright rejection of his friendship.'

'An outright rejection might be preferable to letting the situation linger on until he has become completely besotted,' Lyle pointed out harshly.

'Thank you,' she replied coldly, 'but I'll deal with the situation in my own way, *if* and *when* necessary.'

'Very well,' he said in a tight-lipped manner, 'but if you disrupt him in his studies in any way, then you will have me to deal with.'

The warning was there, and so perfectly clear that it sent a little shiver up her spine, but she refused to be intimidated.

'Yes, sir, Professor Venniker!' She acknowledged his warning sarcastically, but her insides quivered at the blazing fury she saw in his dark eyes when he glanced at her.

They did not speak to each other after that unless it was absolutely necessary, and Christie finally leaned back in her seat and lowered her dark glasses on to her small straight nose. It was hot, and she was tired, but she could not sleep in the Jeep. Her conversation with Lyle had disturbed her more than she wanted to believe, and she could only hope that, once they were back in the city, Dennis's feelings for her would cool rapidly. She did not intend to disrupt his studies, as Lyle seemed to think, and she did not want to hurt him, but she had a feeling it might be inevitable.

There was one other thought that plagued her. Would she see Lyle again? She thought of Sonia Deacon, blonde and beautiful, and a stabbing pain lodged itself in her chest. Sonia would be waiting for him, and Christie imagined that Lyle was equally anxious to get back to Sonia. Why shouldn't he be? Christie tortured herself. Sonia did not have a career which would take her away from Lyle. She would always be there when he needed her. That was one of the accusations Lyle had flung at Christie in that heated argument before he had left for Italy. 'You're never there when I need you!' he had shouted at her, and she had shouted back, 'You should have thought of that before you married someone with a career like mine!'

Raking up the past was painful. She had lost Lyle five years ago, but this time it would be more painful than before. She glanced at him from time to time, but his hawk-like profile remained stern and forbidding. It was impossible to talk to him, or to find some level on which they could communicate without rancour, and the kilometres sped by while they maintained a stony silence.

They stopped for refreshments at Nylstroom, but the lack of frivolity amongst the group told Christie that they shared her sadness at the thought that the expedition had come to an end. They ate their hamburgers and drank their cold drinks in silence, and Christie joined the three girls for a quiet chat to avoid being alone with Dennis when she saw him walking purposefully in her direction.

The last part of their journey seemed to go much faster than the first, and Christie felt a savage tightening in her chest when Johannesburg's skyscrapers came into sight. It was almost time to say goodbye, and she was not looking forward to it.

'Do you need a lift to your flat?' Lyle broke the

strained silence between them when they neared the university grounds, and she shook her head to give herself a moment to control her voice.

'If you drop me off at the nearest bus stop I'll manage.'

'Well, here's a bus stop coming up,' he announced a few seconds later, pulling to the side of the road, and the rest of the convoy came to a halt behind them.

'Thanks,' Christie murmured, jumping out and lifting her bag off the back seat.

'Hey, Christie!' Dennis leapt down from the truck and walked towards her with long, quick strides. 'I haven't got your address.'

Christie's eyes met Lyle's as he walked round the back of the Jeep. She saw the disapproval in his tight-lipped features, but she decided to ignore it for the moment.

'I'm in the telephone book,' she said to Dennis. 'Give me a call sometime.'

Leaving her bag on the pavement, she went to say goodbye to the rest of the group, and several minutes elapsed before she found herself confronting Lyle. The bus was coming, she could see it approaching from the direction they had come, and everything she had planned to say vanished from her mind.

'I suppose this is ... goodbye,' she croaked, swallowing convulsively as the bus drew near and came to a squealing halt in front of the Jeep.

'I'd like you to know that your services were appreciated.'

For one frightful moment she suspected that he was referring to that night they had made love rather than her services as a shorthand/typist, and she hastily picked up her bag to climb into the bus before he noticed the tell-tale warmth surging into her cheeks.

Christie sat down beside a window and, oblivious of the curious glances of the other passengers, she turned in her seat and waved. The students waved back enthusiastically, but Lyle stood with his hands thrust into the pockets of his trousers. There was a strange grimness about his mouth as the bus pulled away with a jolt, and she felt embarrassing tears fill her eyes.

Christie showered and shampooed her hair that night, and she lingered under the jet of warm water for the sheer pleasure of it before she turned off the tap and dried herself. The silk of her nightdress felt good against her perfumed skin after the cheap cotton pyjamas she had worn the past weeks, and she dried her hair with the blow drier before she curled up on her bed with her carved, wooden jewellery box.

She had put this moment off until she had known she would be able to satisfy her curiosity without being disturbed, and her heart was bouncing wildly against her ribs when she turned the small key in the lock. She lifted the lid and slipped her hand inside until her fingers came into contact with a flat, circular object. She took it out and in the palm of her hand lay the ivory disc which Lyle had given her five years ago. She slipped her free hand beneath her pillow and brought out a bright green scarf which she opened carefully to expose the disc she had found. She placed it beside its replica on the palm of her hand, and she felt again that strange excitement churning through her. They were identical except for the figure in the centre, and Christie could not help but admire the craftsman who had made these discs a thousand years ago.

The two discs were both in equally good condition. They were yellowed with age, but other than that they were perfect. They belonged together. If not with two people who loved each other, as Indlovukazi and her lover had loved each other, then in an archaeological museum where the discs would never be parted again.

Christie took out a small blue velvet bag which was not in use, and she carefully dropped the two discs into it. She tightened the satin cord at the opening, and knotted it securely. One day, perhaps, she might find the strength to part with one, or both of these precious discs, but for the moment they were hers, and hers alone.

It was difficult settling down after the weeks of physical exertion. She would have to think of finding another job, but at the same time she toyed with the idea of taking a relaxing holiday to get away from everything, and to get her life back into perspective. Knowing that Lyle was in Johannesburg made it all the more difficult for her to drag her thoughts away from him. It was no use hoping that she would see him again. That night they had made love she had known that she could still attract him physically, but afterwards he had made it quite clear that he no longer cared. He was a man with normal physical needs, he had said, and if she had doubted him in any way, then he had underlined the fact by his reaction to the song she had sung that last night around the camp fire. She meant nothing to him.

The old wounds of the past had been ripped open, and she knew again the pain and misery of having lost the only man she could ever love.

There was no sense in hoping for miracles, but her foolish heart still clung to the fragile hope that Lyle might come back to her.

Three days after her return to Johannesburg, Christie received a cheque in the post and a brief letter from the university thanking her for the service she had rendered. It seemed to her that, with this cheque, all contact with Lyle had been broken, and her misery and longing intensified to the extent that she wept for hours that day.

Sammy Peterson telephoned to welcome her back and he invited her out to lunch, but she refused. She had known him long enough to know what an invitation to lunch would entail. He would have a new, more tempting contract tucked away inside his jacket and, at a given moment, he would produce it with a flourish. Her refusal to sign it would not stop him from rattling off the advantages provided in the contract, and in the end they would part company with Sammy feeling wounded and annoyed that she could have refused the 'golden opportunity' he had offered her.

Christie had been home a week when her doorbell chimed shortly after six one evening and, when she opened the door as far as the safety chain would allow, she was surprised to find Dennis standing there smiling at her rather apologetically.

'I decided to take a chance on finding you at home rather than telephoning,' he explained. 'I hope you don't mind?'

'I don't mind at all,' she assured him, sliding back the safety chain and opening the door wide. 'Come in.'

Tall and lean, he stepped inside, and his green glance briefly scanned her comfortably furnished flat while she closed the door and gestured him into a chair. It was good to see him again, Christie decided as she took in his youthful appearance. The cream-coloured slacks and navy blazer made him look vastly different from the dust-grovelling archaeology student she had come to know, but then, she supposed, she looked different as well in the surroundings which were more familiar to her, and she could see that Dennis was entertaining the same thoughts when his appreciative glance swept her silk-clad figure.

'Do you have anything special planned for this evening?' he asked, lounging comfortably in the chair facing hers.

'No, I don't,' she confessed without thinking.

'That's great, because there is this little place I know of that makes the most fantastic pizzas.' His enthusiasm was replaced by a look of uncertainty. 'You do eat pizzas, don't you?'

Christie's smile of amusement deepened. 'I love them.'

'You'll come with me, then?'

She hesitated, not knowing what to do. Lyle's warnings were still fresh in her mind, but at that moment she did not have the heart to hurt Dennis.

'I'll be with you in a minute,' she promised, and she left him there in the lounge while she touched up her make-up and collected her bag and a wrap.

Dennis's silver-grey Colt was fast and manoeuvrable in the traffic and, when they reached Tony's Pizza Parlour, it slid without effort into a parking space which had only just been vacated.

The pizza parlour seemed crowded, but Dennis

steered Christie towards a vacant table in the far corner. The tempting aroma of pizzas and freshly ground coffee made her realise that she had been wrong in thinking that she was not hungry and, when Dennis placed their order, her mouth actually began to water in anticipation.

The blue, checked tablecloth looked cool and fresh beneath the dim light which hung low over the table, and Christie felt a little awkward until she began to question Dennis about his studies and the conclusive tests which would have to be carried out on the relics they had uncovered. His enthusiasm for archaeology was clearly evident when he told her that it had been ascertained that the relics definitely dated back to the Iron Age. The expedition had been a worthwhile experience, and Lyle's notes on their daily progress had been discussed at length.

'The professor has had extra copies made of your typed scripts so that we can study them at our leisure,' Dennis informed her just as their pizzas and coffee was served.

They ate their pizzas in silence and drank their coffee, but Christie could see that something was troubling Dennis. He smiled at her whenever their glances met, but a slight frown drew his dark brows together when he thought he was unobserved.

The pizza parlour was emptying gradually when Dennis looked up and asked, 'Could I order you another cup of coffee?'

'I still have some, thanks,' she smiled, and that little frown was suddenly back between his brows.

He looked at her, his eyes intent upon her face, and after a moment of obvious indecision he said almost accusingly, 'You haven't asked about the professor.'

'What about him?' she asked, instantly on her guard.

'He's been in a foul mood ever since we came back from that trip,' Dennis enlightened her with a scowl, and Christie hovered somewhere between amusement and concern.

'What do you expect me to do about that?'

'There was a time when he was that someone special in your life,' Dennis reminded her cruelly of the past.

'That was a long time ago.'

'Are you going to tell me about it?'

He looked at her expectantly, but she shook her head with an adamant, 'No.'

She did not want to discuss her marriage to Lyle with anyone, least of all with Dennis. The subject was too personal ... and too painful.

'Is there any chance of you and the professor getting together again?' Dennis interrupted her thoughts while she drank the last of her coffee.

'No chance at all,' she told him, putting down her cup and lowering her lashes to hide the pain in her eyes.

'Then what about you and I——'

'No!' Christie interrupted sharply when she realised what he was about to say. This was what she had feared might happen, and this was what Lyle had warned against, but there was no way to end it other than being firm.

'No?' His green eyes looked hurt and puzzled when he leaned towards her across the table. 'Just like that ... and with no acceptable explanation?'

Christie hated herself at that moment and, filled with remorse, she placed her hand lightly over his. 'Dennis, you're a very nice young man, and I appreciate your friendship, but that's all it will ever be.'

'Are you still in love with Professor Venniker?'

'That's none of your business.' She withdrew her hand from his, but the look on his face made the ice melt around her heart. 'Don't make me hurt you, Dennis, because that's the last thing I would want to do,' she pleaded.

'Just answer one question, Christie, then I shan't pester you again.' There was no laughter in his eyes when they met hers. 'What went wrong between the professor and yourself?'

Everything, she wanted to say, but that would lead to further questions, and she could not bear to discuss the mistakes she had made.

'It was a clash of careers,' she answered carefully, but in a fairly conclusive way. 'His profession took him one way, and mine took me another.'

That summed up the situation perfectly and truthfully, Christie thought as they left the pizza parlour. Lyle's career had taken him to Italy, while hers had taken her on a tour of the country, and the physical and mental distance between them had made a reconciliation impossible.

Five years was a long time of waiting and hoping, and finally resigning herself to the inevitable, but meeting Lyle again had made her realise that there was more than simply a gap of time between them. He had wanted her that night after the incident with the snake, but even during those moments of physical closeness she had been aware of the mental distance between them. God knows, it had been easy to bridge that physical gap, but the mental gap was something quite different, and the closer she had tried to get to him, the more she had discovered that she was simply battering herself senseless against an immovable rock.

'Will I see you again?' Dennis asked hopefully when they arrived at her flat, and the smile that curved her mouth was sympathetic as she shook her head.

'I don't think that would be wise, do you?' she asked gently.

'Does that mean you don't want to see me again?' He scowled down at his shoes.

'I want you to concentrate on your studies, Dennis,' she advised softly, touching his cheek lightly with her fingers and feeling almost maternal. 'If you honestly have nothing more important to do, then you're welcome to drop in for a cup of coffee and a friendly chat.'

Christie wondered afterwards if her offer had not been a little unwise, but she had not been able to bear his downcast expression, and his smile, though sad, had been ample reward.

'Leave him alone,' Lyle had warned, 'or you will have me to deal with.' Lyle was so far removed from her at that moment that his warning carried no impact, but she had, after all, made it quite clear to Dennis that there could never be anything but friendship between them, and he had accepted that. Had he not?

Christie felt unhappy about Dennis, and she felt guilty, too. She had done nothing to attract him, she told herself, but that did not make her feel any better about the situation. During the next few days she almost expected to find Lyle breathing fire at her door, but nothing of the sort happened, and she slowly began to relax.

Her telephone rang one evening, and she thought, 'This is it!' She lifted the receiver, fully expecting Lyle's deep voice to explode in her ear, but she was mistaken.

'This is Sonia Deacon speaking,' a feminine voice purred. 'I imagine Lyle must have told you about me?'

'As a matter of fact, he didn't,' Christie had to prick Sonia's balloon of self-confidence. 'I saw you, though, on the morning we left the university campus to go on the expedition to the northern Transvaal, and one of the students mentioned your name.'

'How thoughtful.'

'Yes, wasn't it?' Christie replied smoothly, wondering what this call was in aid of.

'Perhaps I should explain my reasons for contacting you,' Sonia announced as if she had read Christie's thoughts.

'Perhaps you should.'

'It's about Lyle.'

Christie's mind skidded across a list of various mishaps of which one was more terrifying than the other. Was he ill? Was that what Sonia Deacon wanted to tell her?

'What about him?' she asked with an uninterested calmness which belied the turmoil of anxiety that stormed through her.

'I'm afraid I can't discuss it on the telephone.' That feminine purr intensified Christie's concern to the point of frustration. 'Are you free tomorrow morning?'

'I am.' She would have been free even if she had had to cancel a string of engagements.

'Do you know the Feodora Tea Room in Bree Street?'

Who doesn't, Christie though wryly. When the Feodora Tea Room opened its doors to business a year ago it became an avid topic of conversation. It was the place where wealthy women could rid themselves of their boredom by spending a fortune on tea and scones while they picked up and passed on the latest scandal.

'It's near Garlicks, isn't it?' Christie sought unnecessary confirmation while her mind darted about wildly.

'That's correct,' came the reply. 'Meet me there for tea at eleven.'

The conversation ended on that abrupt note, and Christie was left to wonder what there was about Lyle which was of such importance that Sonia Deacon would actually telephone her with an invitation to tea. There was, however, one small consoling thought. If Lyle had been at death's door, then Sonia would surely have said something to that effect.

There was something else niggling at Christie when she went to bed that night. How had Sonia Deacon found out about her? She could only have heard Lyle mentioning her name, but Christie could not even begin to imagine why Lyle had felt it necessary to discuss her with his current girlfriend.

Christie was more than simply curious, and her curiosity and concern resulted in a restless night during which she tossed her thoughts backwards and forwards through her mind, but without success. Exhaustion finally claimed her in the early hours of the morning, and when she awoke at seven-thirty she had one of those throbbing headaches which persisted despite the amount of pain-killing tablets she had taken.

CHAPTER SEVEN

THE Feodora Tea Room had a blatant elegance about it that matched some of the ladies who frequented it, and the thick pile of the wine-red carpet silenced Christie's footsteps when she stepped inside. She paused a moment, her glance searching amongst the sea of faces for the woman she had seen only briefly some weeks ago, and she was beginning to feel conspicuous when a blue-coated black man stepped from behind the padded counter.

'May I get you a table, madam?'

'I'm here to meet Miss Sonia Deacon,' she explained, and his expression told her he had been warned to expect her.

'This way, madam,' he gestured gallantly with a sweep of his hand, and she was led along an aisle beside a row of tables which had been partitioned off for privacy. He stopped beside the very last table where Sonia awaited Christie, then he bowed politely and returned to the counter at the entrance.

'You're very punctual.' Sonia smiled, but the smile did not reach those cool grey eyes. 'Please sit down.'

'Thank you.'

They sat facing each other across the small round table, and Christie knew that Sonia Deacon was summing her up just as she was taking stock of this blonde, beautiful, and elegantly clad woman who had invited her to the

Feodora for tea and a discussion which concerned Lyle.

'I took the liberty of placing an order, and... Ah, here it comes now,' Sonia broke the silence between them, and a white-aproned waitress served their tea and cream scones in delicate china cups and plates. 'You will have a scone, won't you?' Sonia asked when the waitress had departed. 'Or do you have to watch your weight?'

Christie detected a note of sarcasm in her voice, but she chose to ignore it for the moment. 'My weight has always remained stable no matter what I eat.'

Sonia smiled as she poured their tea, but once again the smile did not reach her eyes. 'Do you take milk?'

'Yes, thank you.'

A cup was passed to Christie and she helped herself to sugar before sampling the cream scone. It was light and fluffy, and the cream was fresh, but at that moment she could not give it the appreciation it deserved. After a sleepless night she was not in a very appreciative mood, and her patience was wearing thin.

'I simply adore coming here,' Sonia purred like a satisfied kitten when they had eaten their scones and were drinking their tea. 'It has such a cosy atmosphere, don't you think?'

'I'm afraid I'm not a connoisseur of tea rooms,' Christie stated rather bluntly, pushing her empty cup aside. 'Look, Miss Deacon, could we forget the platitudes and get down to the reason why you requested this meeting?'

'Very well,' Sonia smiled, her beautiful mouth curving cynically, and her cold eyes meeting Christie's. 'I know you were married to

Lyle some years ago.'

Christie's back stiffened. 'That I have already gathered.'

'I also suspected that it was you who went along as Lyle's secretary on this last expedition with his students, and you confirmed this when I spoke to you on the telephone last night.'

'That's true,' said Christie, recalling her admittance that she had seen Sonia on the university campus. 'You, in turn, said that you wanted to talk about Lyle, and I'm still waiting to discover the reason for this meeting.'

'I am here on Lyle's behalf, and he wants you to stay out of his life in future.'

Christie had asked for it, but the suddenness of it seemed to stun her into disbelief. 'I beg your pardon?'

'You heard me quite clearly, but I'll repeat it if you like.' Sonia's purring voice oozed confidence with a touch of venom. 'Stay away from Lyle. You may have been married to him once, but that does not signify that you have the right to force your unwanted presence on him now.'

Christie could not deny to herself that there was a particle of truth in Sonia's statement. Lyle had given her every indication that he had disliked having her accompany him on that expedition, but she had never dreamed that he would discuss his dislike of her with this woman, and neither had she imagined that he would agree to someone else speaking on his behalf.

'You're making it sound as if I've been flinging myself at him,' Christie protested defensively.

'Isn't that why you applied for that job as his secretary?' Sonia questioned her cynically.

'The job was advertised, and I applied for it

without knowing that Lyle would be the officiating professor,' Christie answered truthfully. 'I had no idea at all that he was back in the country.'

'Do you really expect me to believe that?' Sonia laughed softly, her cynical expression deepening. 'Do you think Lyle believes that it all happened by chance?'

A wave of anger swept through Christie. 'You may both believe what you wish.'

'Are you still in love with him?'

The question was rapped out with a startling swiftness which might have shocked a younger woman into revealing her feelings unwittingly, but Christie met Sonia's cold, calculating glance with a steady, deceptive calmness. 'I respect and admire him very much as an archaeologist, but whatever else I may feel for him is no one's business but my own.'

Sonia leaned back in her chair, her eyes darting chips of ice at Christie, and an ugly, malicious smile twisting her lovely mouth into an uncomplimentary shape. 'In other words you do still love him.'

She was taking a chance on Christie breaking under the strain of her deliberate attack, but Christie was too angry at that moment to feel anything other than an intense dislike for this woman whose outer shell of beauty seemed to peel away to reveal the ugly core beneath.

'I think you have accomplished what you set out to do,' Christie said coldly, her hands gripping her handbag so tightly under the table that her fingers ached. 'Lyle is yours, if you want him that badly, and you have my word that I shan't interfere, or lay the slightest claim on his attention.'

'Lyle will be relieved to hear that,' Sonia purred,

a glittering smile of victory lighting up her eyes for the first time.

'I'm sure he will,' Christie snapped, rising to her feet. 'Thanks for the tea, and goodbye, Miss Deacon.'

Christie was aware of several curious glances directed at her when she walked out of the Feodora, but her head was held high on her squared shoulders, and not for anything in the world would she let anyone guess that she had just been hurt so deeply that she felt more like bursting into tears.

She got into her blue Mazda and drove back to her flat, but she could not recall afterwards how she had got there without committing a traffic offence. She felt numb and cold inside, as if her pain had become a solid block of frozen ice inside her. The water boiled in the kettle, and she made herself a strong cup of tea which she swallowed down hastily. It scalded her mouth, but it also seemed to revive her. She had shed so many tears in the past that she had imagined there were no more tears left, but they poured down her cheeks as if a tap had been opened, and somehow she was incapable of stopping them.

Christie stumbled into her room and made no further attempt to curb her tears. She fell across her bed and said a mental farewell to a crazy dream while she wept until she felt totally drained.

Two days later Christie was still nursing the mental bruises she had obtained during her meeting with Sonia Deacon, and she was in no mood for visitors when her doorbell chimed early that evening. She opened the door as far as the safety chain would allow, and dismay and anger surged through her at the sight of Lyle's tall, lean frame leaning nonchalantly against the door jamb.

What was he doing there? Had he come to warn her once again to leave Dennis alone or was this a social call? Christie could not believe that it was the latter after the assurance Sonia had given her that he would be relieved if she would fade out of his life for good, but neither could she believe that he had come because of Dennis. Lyle's face was partially in shadow, but there was no anger on his hawk-like features.

'What do you want?' she demanded, her voice cold and brittle with annoyance, and the deep timbre of his soft, mocking laughter scraped along nerves that were incredibly raw.

'First of all I'd like to come in, if I may.'

'What for?'

'To talk to you.'

Her insides were shaking and her heart was pounding so loudly that she was certain he could hear it. 'We have nothing to talk about.'

'I can think of quite a few things I'd like to say to you,' he said, and she lowered her gaze before the glitter of mockery in his eyes.

'I'm not interested.' She stepped back, intending to slam the door in his face, but the door would not move and, when she lowered her gaze, she realized why. 'Take your foot out of the door,' she snapped angrily.

'Not until I have your word that you will release the safety chain and let me in.' His compelling glance drew hers like a magnet and he must have read the negative reply in her eyes before she could voice her refusal. 'Christie,' he warned, his manner threatening. 'If you don't let me in I shall create a scene which your neighbours will never let you live down.'

'Damn you, Lyle!' She glared at him, her eyes burning with resentment and anger, but something warned her that he would do exactly as he had threatened, and she sighed helplessly. 'All right, you win.'

'This is much better,' Lyle smiled mockingly when she had released the safety chain and had let him in. 'I like your flat, and I notice you still have most of the furniture we bought together,' he remarked, his dark gaze sweeping the room.

Christie felt her anger boiling up inside her again. 'I'm sure you didn't come here to take an inventory, so say what you have to say, and get out.'

'Are you always this rude to your visitors?' he wanted to know, his eyebrows raised in sardonic amusement.

'I'm not in the mood for visitors, and especially not you,' she answered bitingly, her glance taking in the width of his shoulders beneath the expensive cut of his beige jacket, and the leanness of his hips in the brown slacks. That aura of masculinity which surrounded him was as potent as ever, and she knew that she had to be on her guard against it. 'What do you want, Lyle?'

'To talk, that's all,' he said and, not waiting for an invitation, he sat down in a comfortably padded chair, and stretched his long legs out in front of him.

'If you've come here to stress the fact that you want me out of your life, then you needn't bother,' she said stiffly, her eyes dark with pain and suppressed fury. 'I got the message loud and clear.'

A slight frown appeared between his dark

brows. 'I'm afraid I don't know what you're talking about.'

'You know damn well what I'm talking about!' she almost shouted at him, her body rigid as she stood looking down at him with her hands clenched at her sides. 'You were so concerned that I might want to wriggle my way back into your favour that you sent Sonia to warn me off. What did you tell her, Lyle? Did you tell her that you were glad the expedition was over, and that you hoped I would have the good sense in future to stay away from you? Is that why she arranged to meet me at the Feodora so that she could enlighten me on your behalf as to how you wouldn't tolerate my presence in your life? Were you too much of a coward to face me and tell me that yourself?'

The whiteness of fury settled about his mouth. 'If there was anyone I had to face in that respect, then it was Sonia. I made it quite clear to her a few nights ago that I considered it was time she started focusing her attention on someone else.'

It felt as if the floor had suddenly caved in beneath Christie, and she was left to grope for a new foothold. 'You ended your relationship with her?'

'That's correct.'

She stared at him, trying to probe what lay beneath that harsh exterior. 'I don't believe you.'

'I also told her that she was becoming a positive nuisance, and that I had more important things on my mind ... such as you,' he said blandly, linking his hands behind his dark head, and looking up at her with a gleam of mockery in his eyes. 'Whom you want to believe is your choice entirely.'

Christie still laboured under that feeling that the

breath had been knocked out of her body. She was confused and bewildered, and quite incapable of reasoning sensibly.

'I think I'll go and made some coffee,' she said weakly, and fled into the kitchen.

She switched on the kettle and set out the cups, but her mind was not on what she was doing. Nothing seemed to make sense at that moment. Sonia wanted Lyle so badly that she had gone as far as warning Christie to stay out of his way, but Lyle had contradicted that by saying he had broken off his relationship with Sonia. If Lyle was telling the truth, then Sonia's actions could have been prompted by jealousy. But what if Sonia had spoken the truth?

One thought followed fast and furiously in the wake of another, and the one was more unpalatable than the other until Christie thrust them from her with a shiver of revulsion to concentrate on what she was doing.

Lyle was still lounging in the chair when she returned carrying a tray, but he had removed his jacket, and he was smoking a cigarette which he put out in the ashtray beside him when she handed him his coffee. Christie lowered herself into the chair facing him, but she made no attempt to break the silence between them. She was still too confused, and there were too many doubts still flitting through her mind.

'The work you did for me was excellent,' he surprised her with his praise. 'I can't tell you how grateful I am, and I want to thank you on behalf of the students.'

'You've thanked me already, and there is absolutely no need for your gratitude.' She brushed aside his words with a touch of annoyance. 'I was paid for the job I did, and I did only what was required of me.'

'You did far more than what was required of you,' he corrected her, with that hateful glitter of mockery in his eyes, and for one shattering moment she thought again that he was referring to their lovemaking, then he added, 'it was not part of your job to become actively involved in the excavations.'

She breathed an inward sigh of relief, but her nerves were still quivering with agitation. 'Why didn't you stop me?'

'At first it amused me to watch you, and I wondered how much dust and heat it would take before the novelty would wear off.' The mockery left his eyes and his expression sobered into an unfathomable mask. 'I don't mind admitting that I was ashamed of my uncomplimentary thoughts when you convinced me that you were actually enjoying it.'

'I did enjoy it,' she confessed, relaxing her guard a fraction and absently straightening the skirt of her green floral dress. 'I felt like a child on a treasure hunt, but I was also fascinated at the prospect of uncovering history, and I could seldom wait to take down your notes in the afternoons.'

'You found my notes interesting?' he questioned, his dark eyes narrowed and intent upon her face.

'They were extremely interesting and informative,' she answered truthfully, and that faint light of mockery was suddenly back in his eyes.

'Would you say you have developed a taste for archaeology?'

A reluctant smile plucked at the corners of her mouth. 'Let's just say that what I've always considered a rather dead subject has become a great deal more alive to me.'

A treasure hunt. Her own words skipped through her mind while they drank their coffee. She had found a treasure, had she not? The ivory disc had been united with its replica ... and it was still in her possession. She recalled her guilt at hiding it from Lyle, and she also recalled how, for a fleeting moment, she had thought that Lyle had known it was in her possession. Had it been her imagination, or had he actually suspected she had found Indlovukazi's love-token? Was that perhaps the true reason for his unexpected visit?

Lyle leaned back in his chair, his action startling her out of her guilty reverie, but he merely lit a cigarette. 'Have you found another job yet?' he asked, studying her intently through a cloud of smoke.

'I've applied for a few, but I haven't heard anything to date,' she replied carefully, placing her cup in the tray, and trying desperately to appear relaxed and casual. 'I'm in no hurry, though,' she added.

Anxious for something to do in order to regain her complete composure, Christie offered him another cup of coffee and, when he nodded, she went into the kitchen to pour it. Why was he here? What did he want? Her mind rapped out the queries, but seemed incapable of finding the answers.

'I'm planning an expedition for the next semester,' Lyle informed her when she placed his coffee on the small table beside his chair, and he studied the tip of his cigarette thoughtfully before he glanced up at her questioningly. 'Would you be interested in coming along as my secretary?'

'No!' Her voice was sharp and brittle with rejection as she sat down, but she softened her refusal by adding softly, 'Thanks.'

'I thought your new-found interest in archaeology might make you jump at the chance,' he mocked her derisively, stirring his coffee and swallowing down a mouthful.

'I would love to go,' she admitted, injecting a note of sarcasm into her voice, 'but I think the less we see of each other in future, the better, don't you?'

'I was hoping we could see a great deal more of each other,' he contradicted in an unperturbed manner, and her anger returned with an even greater volume than before.

'Why this sudden interest, Lyle?' she demanded coldly, her eyes twin flames of blue fury. 'When we met on the campus six weeks ago you were furious at discovering that I was to be your secretary during the expedition, and afterwards you made it quite clear that you couldn't stand the sight of me.'

'Did I really?' he drawled with infuriating mockery.

'You know you did,' she spat out the words. 'You seldom spoke to me unless you absolutely had to.'

'As I recall, we had several very interesting conversations.'

'They were conversations during which you did your best to insult and humiliate me,' she reminded him bitterly. 'And what about that *total indifference* you once mentioned?'

'I spoke rashly and in a moment of anger, but I disproved it later, didn't I?'

Christie inhaled sharply through her teeth. This

time there was no mistake about his deliberate reference to something she would rather have forgotten. Her resistance had been low, and in that vulnerable state he had taken advantage of her. No, she could not blame him entirely, her conscience warned. She had not needed very much encouragement to surrender herself to him, and she had to carry an equal share of the guilt.

'We were both caught up in the aftermath of that terrifying experience with the mamba,' she said at length, shuddering inwardly at the memory and brushing aside the matter with a forced casualness. 'It meant nothing.'

'Didn't it?' He crushed his cigarette into the ashtray and pinned her to her chair with a fiery glance. 'I think it meant a lot more than we're both prepared to admit.'

'It proved, perhaps, that we are still physically attracted to each other,' she agreed sarcastically, 'but that's all.'

His mouth twisted with stabbing derision. 'Wouldn't you consider that a good enough start on which to base a new relationship?'

'Are you perhaps suggesting that I should become your ... your mistress?' she demanded, her cheeks flaring with indignation.

'I gather the idea doesn't appeal to you,' he smiled twistedly.

'It doesn't appeal to me at all,' she retorted coldly, leaping agitatedly to her feet and walking across to the window to draw a breath of sanity while she stared down into the busy street where the neon signs flashed an invitation to the entertainment seekers.

'What would you suggest, then?' Lyle's deep voice continued to mock her, and she knew that she had stretched her composure and her hospitality as far as it would go for one evening.

'I suggest you finish your coffee, and go home.'

There was an absolute and almost electrifying silence before she heard Lyle get up and move away from his chair. She waited for the sound of the door opening and closing, but instead she felt him coming up behind her. Every nerve was stretched taut and quiveringly alive to his nearness, and her heart was beginning to hammer against her ribs like a wild bird seeking release. She was trapped between him and the window, and she did not want to turn and face him. She needed time to control her expression if she did not want him to see the pain and disappointment in her eyes.

'Christie . . .' His voice was low and vibrant, and his hands touched her shoulders in something close to a caress, sending an exquisite warmth flowing into her body through the silk of her dress. 'Let's talk sensibly and seriously without taking a verbal dig at each other all the time.'

He was so close to her that her senses were tantalised by the woody scent of his masculine cologne, and every fragment of her resentment was demolished as if it had never existed. 'I think we have forgotten how to speak decently to each other.'

'If we put a little effort into it I'm sure we could succeed,' he murmured, drawing her against him so that her back came to rest against his broad, solid chest, and a familiar weakness surged through her when she felt his breath stirring the short hair in the nape of her neck.

'Could we?' she heard herself asking in a breathless voice which did not seem to belong to her. 'Could we succeed?'

'We could start off by trying to be honest with each other,' Lyle suggested, his hands moving in an achingly sweet caress against her shoulders, and down her arms.

How honest could they be with each other? she wondered. How honest dared they be while there was still the fear of being hurt?

'There is something I have to know.' Her voice was a little unsteady when she turned beneath his hands, and she had to look a long way up before her probing glance met his. 'Why did you behave as if you hated the very sight of me?'

'Seeing you again after so many years brought back, with a vengeance, all the anger and bitterness of the past.' He smiled at her as he raised a hand to brush the back of his fingers against her cheek in a familiar caress, but his eyes remained shuttered, and she had the oddest feeling that he had not told her the absolute truth. 'It also made me realise that I still wanted you,' he added softly, his smile deepening with a sensuality that made her pulse quicken.

There was no mention of love; there never had been. She had been so madly in love with him all those years ago that she had believed blindly that he had loved her, too, but she knew now that she had been living in a paradise of her own making He had said *I want you*, and he had followed it up with an offer of marriage, knowing that there was no other way she would get into bed with him, but this time he obviously found the encumbrance of marriage unnecessary. He still wanted her in the physical sense and, since she had been fool enough to fall into his bed with despicable eagerness that night at the camp, he naturally considered that she would be happy to oblige him again.

Her throat was achingly tight, and she turned away from him without speaking before he saw that glimmer of tears in her eyes which she was trying so desperately to blink away. She could hear Lyle speaking to her, but it took several seconds before she actually registered what he was saying.

'I've been wanting to talk to you since our return two weeks ago. It's important that we come to some amicable agreement about our future, but I've been bogged down with the analysis of the items we brought back with us, and there have been lectures and endless discussions.' He was silent for a moment, then he spun her round to face him and demanded, exasperated, 'Christie, are you listening to me?'

She swallowed convulsively and forced herself to meet his stabbing glance. 'I'm listening.'

His eyes were pin-points of fire raking her face, and his glance lingered on her full, sensitive mouth when it began to quiver with the effort to control her feelings. His hands framed her face, his thumbs moving in a caress across her cheekbones, then he pushed his fingers gently through her golden-brown hair which had grown almost to shoulder length during the past weeks.

'Don't cut your hair again,' he changed the subject in an oddly slurred voice, and Christie was beyond speech as pleasurable sensations cascaded through her at the touch of his fingers against her scalp.

He knew too much about her; he knew exactly how to arouse her with the sensuality of his touch, and if she did not break away from him now she would be lost. She placed her hands against his chest to push him away, but somehow her fingers slid between the buttons of his shirt, and the warmth of his hair-roughened skin against her fingertips sent a surging current of emotions through her that robbed her of the will to do anything. His face became a blur as he lowered his head, and quite suddenly she was aching for the touch of his warm mouth against hers. His lips teased and tantalised, filling her with an urgency that made her mouth move encouragingly beneath his in an exchange of sensually erotic kisses. She was vaguely aware of his warm hands sliding down her back in a slow, practised caress until her body seemed to melt into the curve of his hard frame, but a tiny spark of sanity invaded her mind when she became aware of his heated desire. If she waited too long she would be incapable of controlling her own emotions, and there was one thing she was very sure of at that moment. She did not want him on this 'no strings attached' basis.

'No, Lyle!' Her voice was husky, and she was breathing jerkily when she pushed him away with a burst of strength she had not known she possessed. 'If—if we're going to start a new relationship, then I think we—we should take it slowly.'

He looked momentarily startled, then he lifted an eyebrow in a hint of sardonic amusement. 'How slowly do you intend us to take it?'

Christie was torn in two. Her mind was thinking rationally, but her body seemed to have a mind of its own at that moment, and there was confusion in her body at the delay of what it considered a natural procedure, but her rational-thinking mind won the battle.

'I'd like us both to be sure that this is what we really want,' she said eventually, incapable of meeting his eyes.

'I know what I want, Christie,' The deep timbre of his voice thrilled her. 'How long will it take you to be sure of what *you* want?'

'I—I don't know.' Her mind was confused again, and she gestured helplessly with her hands. 'Please, Lyle, give me time to sort myself out.'

He stood facing her with his thumbs hooked into the belt hugging his slacks to his lean hips, and she wondered if he was annoyed with her. What if he would not wait? What if he walked out of her life again, and never came back?

'If you need time, then I won't push you unnecessarily,' He interrupted her frantic thoughts, and she sighed inwardly with relief when his warm hands framed her face and tilted it up to his. 'Don't take too long, though.'

'I'll try not to.'

Her voice had been a whisper of choked sound, and her eyes filled with embarrassing tears. She expected him to mock her, but instead he brushed her tears away with his lips, and kissed her mouth with a lingering gentleness that made her tremble with the sweetness of it.

'I'll see you tomorrow evening,' he promised and, carrying his jacket over his shoulder, he walked out of her flat and closed the door firmly behind him.

CHAPTER EIGHT

CHRISTIE'S life took on a new dimension during the weeks following their decision to build up a new relationship between them, and at times she could almost make herself believe that Indlovukazi's powers had lingered through the ages to reunite her with Lyle as she had reunited the ivory discs. Perhaps there was some magic in them after all. It was foolish to believe this, but she felt as if she had been given a second chance, and all that remained was for her to make the right decision.

Christie saw Lyle whenever he was free. They dined out often, or went to the theatre, and at weekends they would sometimes take a long drive out into the country. She knew that he had bought himself a house in one of the élite suburbs of Johannesburg, but he did not invite her to his home, and neither did she want him to. It was as if they had come to an unspoken agreement to avoid being alone together in places where they might find themselves incapable of resisting the temptation to see a closer relationship. Lyle had agreed not to push her for a decision she was not ready to make, and he had kept his word despite his noticeable impatience.

It was, for both of them, a period of wanting to get to know each other all over again. It felt strange, but Christie had not needed this time to discover that Lyle was not the same man she had once been married to. He had always possessed a certain element of cynicism, but it had become harsher over the years, and this disturbed her. They had also agreed to be honest with each other, but somehow they never discussed the past, or delved deeper than the surface reasons for the failure of their marriage.

She was also aware of the growing sensation that she stood accused of something which she had no knowledge of. At odd times she had found Lyle staring at her, and the accusation in his eyes had been unmistakable. She had questioned him about it, but he had merely smiled cynically and changed the subject. Was it something she had done, or was it something she had neglected to do? She taxed her mind, forcing herself to cover every particle of ground in their past and present relationship, but nothing came to light. The feeling persisted however and, at times, it drove her crazy with frustration and helplessness.

A growing uneasiness was yet another disturbing factor Christie had to cope with. It grew in momentum with every passing day like a premonition of something yet to come and, like a festering wound, it came to an unexpected head one evening when her doorbell chimed.

'Sammy!' she exclaimed, staring at the stockily built man with the shining bald pate. 'This is a surprise.'

'You think so?' he smiled as she let him in, but his smile was somewhat censorious. 'I believe it is said that, if Mohammed will not come to the mountain, then the mountain will have to come to Mohammed.'

'I'm sorry, Sammy,' she apologised a little guiltily. 'I've been rather busy lately.'

'You have been too busy to visit an old friend, but you haven't been too busy to have dinner and go to the theatre with your ex-husband,' he accused reprovingly. 'Is that not so?'

'How did you find out about Lyle?' she asked, her feelings hovering somewhere between surprise and anger.

'Contacts, darling,' he smiled triumphantly, thrusting one of his favourite cigars between his teeth and lighting it. 'I have many contacts in this city, and you know how easily people talk.'

Yes, she knew and, although she had not purposely wanted to hide the fact that she was seeing Lyle, it still succeeded in annoying her that the information had reached Sammy. 'I wish people would mind their own business!'

'Now, don't get angry, darling.' Sammy warned with that same triumphant smile of a moment ago. 'I have also heard a little rumour that Lyle Venniker was the leader of that expedition you went on.'

Christie should have been used to this sort of thing, but it still succeeded in catching her off guard.

'That's quite true,' she confirmed warily.

'Did you know this when you applied for the job?' Sammy asked, sending a cloud of cigar smoke towards the ceiling, and Christie's blood-pressure rose by several degrees. This was the second time within a few short weeks that someone had referred in some way to the fact that she might have been aware of Lyle's presence on that expedition, and it was becoming a bit too much to tolerate.

'No, I didn't know,' she answered coldly, and another cloud of cigar smoke emerged from Sammy's smiling mouth.

'Can I believe you, darling?'

Sonia's disbelief had been acceptable to a degree, but Sammy's was downright irritating and annoying. 'Have I ever lied to you, Sammy?'

'Not that I can recall, my dear,' he said, taking the cigar out of his mouth and wiping the moistness in the corner of his lips with his handkerchief. 'But there is always a first time.'

'Until the moment we met on the university campus I was convinced that Lyle was still out of the country.' Her voice was cold with fury, and so were her eyes. 'That's the truth, and you can take it, or leave it.'

'You're getting angry again,' he warned, his eyes twinkling with mirth, 'but I don't really mind when it makes your eyes sparkle the way they used to on the stage.' She dismissed his remark with a disparaging gesture of her hands, but Sammy was persistent. 'You were always so alive on the stage when you were singing, Christie, and it breaks my heart to know that now you are simply existing.'

Christie suppressed the desire to laugh at this exaggeration, and said stiffly, 'I'm quite happy with my life the way it is.'

'More so, perhaps, now that Lyle Venniker has arrived back on the scene?'

Her back stiffened with displeasure at this intrusion on her personal life. 'I don't wish to discuss the subject.'

'Don't be a fool once again, darling,' Sammy laughed cynically. 'He's not the man for you, and he won't think twice about walking out on you again.'

'It's entirely up to me whether I want to take that chance or not,' she argued, and Sammy's cigar almost fell out of his gaping mouth.

'You are not thinking seriously of taking him back, are you?'

Christie felt ashamed of herself, but at that moment she actually found herself enjoying his obvious agitation, and she took her time before she said calmly, 'I'm considering it.'

'My God!' he exclaimed, slapping his palm characteristically against his forehead. 'How can you do this to me!'

'What do you mean, how can I do this to you?' she asked, a slight frown marring her smooth brow.

'You are going to tie yourself once again to a man who does not understand the art of self-expression, and he will continue to convince you that you should smother your natural, God-given talent.'

Stay calm! Christie warned herself, but the unfairness of Sammy's statement made her feel as if her anger had been turned on to a slow boil. There was not one occasion that she could recall Sammy saying something complimentary about Lyle, but he had never before voiced his unflattering opinion quite so openly. That feeling of uneasiness, like a premonition, was becoming very strong, and it made her wonder about many things as she recalled the silent, but tangible antagonism which had existed between Sammy and Lyle.

'Lyle had nothing to do with the termination of my career as a singer, if that's what you mean,' she said in defence of the man she loved. 'I was the one who ended it three years ago, and my decision was not influenced by anyone in particular.'

'It was a mistake.' Sammy proffered his unwanted opinion bluntly.

'I'm not so sure of that,' she murmured, ending their conversation for the moment by going into the kitchen to make coffee.

Being alone for a few minutes was thereapeutic. Sammy's personality had always been rather overpowering, and she had seldom emerged from a meeting with him without feeling mentally exhausted. This occasion was no different from the others, and she made use of this opportunity to strengthen her defences against that familiar ritual which she was beginning to despise. She knew Sammy too well, and she did not need to be clairvoyant to know that, tucked away somewhere in his jacket pocket, was a contract waiting for the right moment when Sammy would produce it with his usual flourish.

Christie carried the tray of coffee through to the lounge and, while she poured, she did her best to steer the conversation along a different avenue to the one she feared it would take. She succeeded, but only for as long as it took Sammy to drink his coffee.

'Christie, I have something for you,' he said, his rounded features set with determination as he put his empty cup aside. 'It is an opportunity you cannot afford to cast aside as you have done with the others.'

She raised her hands in an unconsciously physical attempt to ward off the inevitable. 'If it's another contract, then I don't——'

'It is most definitely another contract, darling,' Sammy interrupted her, leaving his cigar burning in the ashtray to produce the document from the inner pocket of his dark grey jacket. 'But this time I want you to consider it seriously.'

'Sammy, I'm not——'

'Wait until I have explained it to you before you think of turning it down,' he interrupted her again with a rebuke in his voice. 'There is no harm in that, is there?'

Whether she relented, or not, it would make no difference to this forceful man, and she gestured helplessly with her hands. 'Go ahead,' she sighed.

His triumph was obvious when he settled himself comfortably in his chair and unfolded the document in his hands. 'What I have here is a recording contract for four albums a year for the next three years.' His smile was confident as he tapped the paper with his fingers. 'Now, how much of your time will it take to record four albums a year?'

There was a catch there somewhere. There always was. Recording four albums a year would not take up much of her time, but one thing always led to another and, before she could prevent it, she would find herself caught up in that same network of binding commitments which had stifled her in the past.

'What about personal appearances?'

'There will be no personal appearances, and no tours unless you agree to it, darling,' he assured her. 'I can guarantee it.'

Christie accepted that with the cynical disbelief it deserved. 'You said that once before and, when I asked you to cancel the tour you were planning for me so that I could accompany my husband on a trip north, you thrust a contract under my nose, and read out a paragraph which I had not fully understood when attaching my signature to it.'

'This time it will be different.'

'Will it?' she laughed bitterly.

'Of course, darling,' he assured her, leaning forward to thrust the document into her unwilling hands. 'Here's the contract, read it, take it to your lawyer, and then decide whether you will accept it or reject it, but you must remember that this is a chance in a million.'

She fingered the contract as if it were something lethal, and she had great difficulty in not tossing it back at him in disgust. Experience had taught her that Sammy Peterson would never cease pestering her if she did not at least agree to reading the contract before rejecting it and, as in the past, she heard herself saying, 'I'll read it, but I'm not promising anything.'

'Good!' he exclaimed, rubbing his hands together with glee as if she had already penned her name to the document. 'I knew you wouldn't disappoint me.'

The doorbell chimed for the second time that evening, and Christie's heart leapt into her throat, shutting off her breath momentarily.

'Excuse me a moment,' she croaked, placing the document on the table beside her chair and rising to her feet.

Her insides were quivering like an animal sensing danger when she walked towards the door. It was Lyle ... she knew it. She also knew, from past experience, that to put these two men in the same room was like tempting fate. Her hand shook when she opened the door and, despite her nervousness, she could not suppress that thrill of pleasure at the sight of Lyle's tall, lean frame.

'I wasn't expecting you this evening,' she smiled up at him, but she had a feeling that her smile was a little twisted.

Lyle's dark glance went beyond her, and his

mouth tightened ominously. 'Have I come at an inopportune moment?'

'No, of course you haven't,' Christie contradicted hastily, taking his arm and drawing him inside. 'I'm very glad you're here.'

The latter was quite true. She hoped that Lyle's presence might help to convince Sammy that she was no longer interested in a singing career, and she also hoped that it would encourage Sammy to leave.

'Ah, Professor Venniker!' Sammy exclaimed, rising to his feet with his cigar protruding once again from the corner of his smiling mouth. 'I suppose it was inevitable that we should meet again now that you're back in the country.'

The dislike between these two men was so intense that it was almost tangible. There was a time when, for her sake, they had made an attempt to be polite to each other, but this time she sensed that there would be no pretence.

'I would have thought a meeting between us quite unlikely, but then I overlooked the fact that people don't change much over the years,' Lyle responded harshly to the obvious sarcasm in Sammy's remark. 'I should have remembered that while there was still a suggestion of glitter left on Christie's star, you would cling to it in order to bask in its glow.'

Christie tried to smooth over the situation by placing a calming hand on Lyle's arm. 'Lyle, please don't make——'

'You are quite right, Professor Venniker,' Sammy interrupted her sharply, 'but there is one factor you have obviously ignored. If it were not for people like myself, then artists such as Christie might end up wasting their talents in spheres where their potential value is not appreciated, and you are one of those unfortunate people who has never had the ability to appreciate talent.'

'Sammy!' Christie gasped, shocked and angry at his deliberate and insulting attack.

'I can appreciate talent,' Lyle hit back in a controlled, but icy voice, 'but I can't appreciate the blood-suckers who deny people like Christie the freedom of choice, and the privilege to enjoy a private life of her own.'

'Are you calling me a blood-sucker?' Sammy shouted, taking his cigar out of his mouth and going a slight shade of purple with anger. *'Me? Sammy Peterson?'*

'Please stop it, both of you!' Christie begged, trying to intervene verbally and physically in this volcanic disagreement, but Lyle placed his hands on her shoulders in a bruising grip and set her aside firmly.

'Yes, I am calling you a blood-sucker,' Lyle continued in that calm, mutinous voice she knew so well. 'You'll take everything you can get out of Christie until she has nothing more to give, and you don't care if you ruin her life in the process.'

'Ruin her life?' Sammy exploded, almost choking on the cigar smoke he had inhaled, and Christie could see the veins jutting out dangerously against his temples.

'Please, Sammy!' she pleaded for the sake of his health more than anything else at that moment, but Sammy ignored her with an angry wave of his hand.

'I took Christie out of that stuffy little coffee bar where she was singing night after night for a mere pittance,' he shouted at Lyle, 'and I made her into one of the best folk singers this country has ever known. She had a good life until you came into it and ruined everything with your selfish attitude.'

'Sammy ... Lyle!' she cried in a choked voice, making a final and desperate attempt to halt the argument between these two men. '*Please* will you stop this!'

'Every man has the right to be selfish once in a while where his marriage is concerned and, considering the facts, I think I was more lenient than most,' Lyle ignored her plea as he towered over Sammy in a threatening manner. 'Christie and I were married for six months and if I had to add the days we spent together, then they would add up to no more than *three months*.'

Christie's mind felt as if it wanted to explode with Lyle's calculations. She had never thought of it that way before, but it was true. They may have been married for six months, but the time they had spent together could not have been more than three. It was a shocking discovery, and she blamed herself for it.

'Was it my fault your careers had such conflicting schedules?' Sammy interrupted her thoughts with his sarcastic query.

'No, it wasn't your fault,' Lyle conceded coldly, 'but you could have helped a little to ease the situation.'

The two men glared at each other like two angry, snarling jungle cats facing each other in an arena. Lyle was physically superior, but Sammy was as cunning as a jackal. He knew how and where to strike, and he would not hesitate to do so.

Sammy gestured disparagingly with the hand that held the cigar. 'I did the best I could under the circumstances.'

'Your best was not nearly good enough,' Lyle hit back.

Christie stared from one to the other in helpless despair. Nothing was working out as she had hoped it would, and that premonition of danger was rising with a chilling force that made her hands feel icy when she clutched at the back of a chair for support.

'I have always tried only to do what is best for Christie, *and* for her career,' Sammy defended himself.

'Have you?' Lyle demanded cynically.

Sammy ignored Lyle and turned to face Christie. 'Haven't I always taken care of you, and haven't I just succeeded in securing you the best contract since your last one expired three years ago, darling?'

'Contract?' Lyle latched on to the word with a savage snarl as if it were something obnoxious.

'Lyle...' she began, wanting desperately to explain, but she was incapable of finding the right words in that moment of stress.

'Read it!' Sammy instructed, waving the document at Lyle. 'It is an opportunity she knows she cannot afford to ignore, and this time her career will be an even greater success than before.'

Christie felt a numb fear surging through her. Sammy had made it sound as if she had already agreed to sign the contract and, when she looked up into Lyle's dark, accusing eyes, she knew with terrifying certainty that he was thinking exactly what Sammy had wanted him to think.

'I don't wish to read it!' Lyle snarled at Sammy, brushing aside the hand that waved the contract at him.

'Lyle, I——' The words locked in Christie's

throat when Lyle silenced her abruptly with an imperious wave of his hand.

'I butted in on a business discussion which doesn't particularly interest me,' he said and, turning towards the door, he added a curt, 'Good night.'

Christie's slender, trembling body leapt into action at last, and she gripped his arm to detain him. 'Lyle, you don't understand, I——'

'Forget it, Christie!' he barked savagely, brushing her restraining hand away with an equally savage action, and his eyes blazed down into hers with such a wealth of hatred in their depths that she fell back a pace. 'I played second fiddle to your binding career once before, but I don't intend to do so again.'

He walked out and slammed the door in her white face with a force that made her flinch, and she stood there for some time staring blindly at the door before she turned away with a weary sigh. It was as if she had watched the replay of an action which had occurred more than five years ago, but this time it was accompanied by the suffocating fear that he would *never* come back.

'Did you have to show Lyle that contract, Sammy?' she asked tiredly of the man who stood observing her with a look of triumph on his round features. 'Did you have to make it sound so definite?'

'It was the best way to judge his character, darling.' He brushed aside her queries. 'If he had cared about you he would have been pleased and happy for you, but instead he was thinking only of himself.'

If he had cared. The words reverberated through her mind. A few revealing truths had emerged during the heated argument between Lyle and Sammy, and Christie was convinced that Lyle had cared sufficiently not to want Sammy to ruin her life. Sammy had been driven into a corner, and then he had played his trump card. He had waved the contract about, creating a false impression, and Lyle had quite naturally jumped to the wrong conclusion.

'Oh, God!' she moaned, subsiding into a chair and burying her white, quivering face in her hands. If only Lyle had given her the opportunity to explain. 'If only...

'Didn't I say he was selfish?' Sammy interrupted her turbulent thoughts, but she ignored his insinuating query. Lyle could be accused of many things, but never selfishness.

'He wouldn't even let me explain,' she whispered in despair, lowering her hands and sagging tiredly in her chair.

'What is there to explain, my dear?'

Christie looked up into Sammy's smiling face and saw there a callousness she had never noticed before. She had always imagined that Sammy cared about her as a person, but she was beginning to suspect that there was a great deal more truth in what Lyle had said. He had, perhaps, seen through Sammy from the very beginning, but she had been too blind to see anything except what she had wanted to see, and now it was too late. *Too late!* The words injected a fire into her veins, and her anger erupted with a new burst of energy.

'I'm not signing that contract, Sammy.' She picked up the document he had dropped on to the table beside her chair, and she stood up to face him squarely as she thrust the contract into his hands. 'I don't even want to read it.'

'Darling, don't be hasty,' Sammy warned, his sublime confidence fanning her anger. 'Think it over carefully, and then let me know how you feel about it.'

'I know exactly how I feel about it.'

I detest it! she could have said, but instead she remained silent, her blue gaze steady and cool as it held Sammy's. He was beginning to look uncomfortable and, for the first time, he appeared to lack his usual suave, confident exterior, but people like Sammy Peterson never gave up easily.

'I'll leave the contract with you,' he said, dropping it on to the coffee table and walking quickly towards the door.

'I don't want it!' Christie shouted, her temper exploding, and she flung the contract at him so that it missed his head by inches and slammed into the door.

Sammy turned to stare at her with wide, uncertain eyes. Christie knew that this was a side of her which he had never encountered before. She had always been docile, like soft putty which he could mould to his liking, but this time she was a desperate woman who had been driven too far.

'I don't want your contract!' she threw at him, stressing her refusal, and wishing he would go and leave her alone.

'Do me a favour, Christie,' Sammy said, rallying swiftly and picking up the document which had lain on the carpeted floor at his feet. 'Just read it, and I'll call you in a couple of days.'

He placed the contract on the telephone table beside the door and left, and she was alone at last.

Christie started shaking. She was shaking so much that she had difficulty in locking the door and sliding the safety chain into position. She had never been this angry and disappointed before. Sammy had insulted Lyle, and he had deliberately placed a new barrier between Lyle and herself. Lyle, on the other hand, should have given her the opportunity to explain how she felt about the contracts Sammy periodically pestered her to sign, but instead he had jumped to the obvious conclusion, and he had left Sammy victorious by walking out on her.

Damn, Sammy! And *damn* Lyle for not trusting her a little more. If she had to decide who was to blame for ruining her life, then they were both equally guilty, and in that moment of anger she mentally washed her hands of both of them.

She was still fuming quietly when she was lying in bed that night, but her anger vanished when she switched off the light, and she found herself lying there in the darkness fighting against a depression which seemed to weigh her down. She felt lonely and miserable, but she was not going to wallow in self-pity. She had to think. She had to decide about her future, and she would have to do so without being influenced by her emotions, but somehow her mind was in a ruthless turmoil of indecision that gave her no peace during the long, dark hours before dawn.

CHAPTER NINE

DENNIS arrived at Christie's flat a week later, and he found her looking like a ghost of her former self. Pale and hollow-eyed, Christie invited him in, and he followed her silently into the kitchen. She was glad that he had come, she decided while she made coffee. He was someone to talk to, and someone to laugh with, but the problem was that she had a stronger desire to cry.

She was aware of Dennis's eyes following her as she moved about her small kitchen, and she knew why. No matter how skilfully she had applied her make-up, she could not disguise the evidence of her sleepless nights, and Dennis was an observant and shrewd young man.

'Have you been ill?' he asked eventually, coming up beside her and leaning against the cupboard to observe her intently.

'No, I haven't.' She tried to evade his question. 'I haven't been sleeping too well lately, but that's nothing unusual.'

'Are you worried about something?'

'Why should I be worried about anything?' she counter-questioned evasively, but she could feel that she was weakening.

'You can answer that question better than I can,' he said, watching her while she poured their coffee and added milk to it. 'I was merely thinking that it helps sometimes to talk to a friend who is impartial.' He leaned closer to her so that she was forced to meet his glance. 'You can trust me,

Christie, you know that, don't you?'

'I know,' she smiled slightly, touching his cheek lightly with her fingers, but her delicate features sobered the next instant, and her eyes mirrored her torment. 'God knows, I suppose I need someone to talk to if I don't want to go slightly crazy,' she heard herself confessing.

'Let's take our coffee through to the lounge, then you can tell me all about it,' he suggested, and Christie did not argue as she led the way out of the kitchen.

She did not want to burden anyone with her problems, least of all Dennis, but her resistance was low, and somehow he succeeded in wheedling the truth out of her. Bit by agonising bit, she found herself telling him almost everything from the first moment she had met Lyle. Once she had started she found that she could not stop, and it poured from her lips like matter escaping from a festering wound to ease some of the pain. If she had expected Dennis to be shocked at the discovery that she had once been married to Lyle, then she was disappointed. He took the news calmly, and he quietly encouraged her to continue until she had reached the point where Lyle had walked out of her flat a week ago.

Dennis had lapsed into a thoughtful silence, then he looked up at her and asked bluntly, 'Do you blame the professor for thinking you were going to sign that contract?'

'No,' she shook her head miserably, 'but I do blame him for not giving me the opportunity to explain.'

'Perhaps he's just as afraid as you are of being hurt a second time.'

'Perhaps,' she agreed, her mind bouncing his

theory about, but without much success. 'I'm so confused, and I wish I knew what to do,' she groaned, pressing her fingers against her tired eyes.

'Have you thought of going to him and explaining everything?'

'I've telephoned three times in an attempt to speak to him, but he was either out, or in conference with someone.' A cynical smile twisted her lovely mouth. 'I left a message, asking him to contact me, but I imagine it was too much to hope for that he would respond, or come to me when he must know that he has been too hasty in his judgment.'

'The professor has his pride, and so have you, it seems,' Dennis said, placing a harsh finger on the core of the problem. 'One of you will have to overcome that obstacle, and the obvious one is you.'

'Haven't I tried?' she demanded indignantly.

'Perhaps you haven't tried hard enough, Christie.' He slammed the ball back into her court. 'I think you and the professor haven't been honest with each other, and if you love him enough, then you can't let pride stand in your way.'

'You think I should bury what little pride I have left and go on my knees to him?'

Dennis's green gaze met hers challengingly. 'If you want him enough you'll go to him and clear up this misunderstanding between you.'

Christie had come to this same conclusion often enough during those long sleepless hours, but her awful pride, and a gnawing fear, had always made her cast aside the thought. 'What if he rejects me?'

'What if he doesn't?' Dennis bounced back. 'Could you live with the uncertainty of never knowing? Could you cope with the knowledge that you never tried?'

She considered this for a moment and felt herself shrink inwardly. 'What you're saying makes sense, but that doesn't prevent me from being afraid.'

'If you want something badly enough you ought to go all out to get it,' he argued. 'How badly do you want the professor?'

Christie could not answer him immediately. He had asked her a question which she had not paused to ask herself during the agonising hours of the past week, but now she was being forced to delve a little deeper into her soul for the answer.

'I want him so badly that I gave up my career three years ago because it meant nothing to me without him, and I've always hoped that somehow ... someday ... he would come back to me,' she said at length, and her hyacinth-blue eyes were shimmering with tears she could not hide.

'If you had the courage to give up your career,' Dennis concluded quietly, 'then you shouldn't have a problem overcoming your pride and fear of confronting him.'

Christie stared at him through a blur of hot tears. It was strange how everything had suddenly shifted into place, and it had taken someone like Dennis to help her get things into perspective. She had selfishly thought only of herself, and she had never taken into consideration that Lyle also had *his* pride. She could not blame him for thinking the worst. She had let him down once before because of the rigid demands her career had made on her, and it was obvious now that the next move had to be hers. If he rejected her, then she would at least have the satisfaction of knowing that she had tried, but, while there was still a slim chance that he would accept her explanation, there was hope.

'Thank you,' she whispered shakily when Dennis got up to leave, and she rose quicky to kiss him briefly on the cheek.

He looked taken aback. 'What are you thanking me for?'

'For everything,' she told him sincerely, 'but most of all for being such a good friend.'

Christie was left with a lot to think about, and there was a great deal of pain involved in her self-analysis. When Lyle had walked out on her five years ago she had had no choice but to let him go, but this time she was in a position to do something about it. It was only fair that she should go to Lyle and explain to him how wrong he had been in thinking that she had contemplated signing that contract and, regardless of how he felt about her, she had to tell him somehow that she loved him.

She was impatient now to get it over with before her courage failed her, and she glanced up at the digital wall-clock in the kitchen. It was eight-fifteen, and still early enough to take a drive out to Lyle's home, but she hesitated. Her pride was finding a list of plausible reasons why she ought not to go, and she wasted precious seconds fighting a silent battle with herself while she rinsed the cups and left them in the rack to dry. She had to see Lyle; she had to clear the air between them, and it was that thought which helped her to emerge the victor.

She entered her bedroom at a running pace to put on a warm jacket and to check her make-up, but nervousness suddenly knotted her insides. Explaining to Lyle about the contract was going to be easy, but telling him that she loved him was going to take a great deal more courage than she possessed at that moment.

Her fingers fiddled absently with the gold pendant hanging about her throat, and her eyes absently followed the action in the mirror, but the next instant an incredible idea took shape in her mind. The ivory discs! She would take them with her and, if she gave Lyle the appropriate one, he would know at once what she was trying to tell him, and this would give her the opportunity to explain how she had found the matching disc.

Excitement boosted her courage and, with the blue velvet pouch in her jacket pocket, she left her flat and took the lift down to the basement where her Mazda was parked. She drove through the busy, well-lit city streets, and out towards the suburb where Lyle lived. She knew the address, but finding it in the dark took most of her concentration and left her no time to rehearse what she was going to say.

The lights were on in Lyle's Tudor-style home, but for some inexplicable reason Christie decided to park her car at the gate and to walk along the curved path to the front entrance. The driveway lay to her left, and through the privet hedge she glimpsed a car parked there which did not belong to Lyle. She hesitated. Perhaps she should have telephoned rather than bursting in on him like this when he obviously had visitors.

Indecision made her pause at the foot of the steps leading up to the door with the stained-glass windows above it. Had she come this far only to turn back? Would she have the courage to bring herself this far again? Too much time had been wasted already, she decided firmly, and she was not going to waste another minute if she could help it.

Christie ascended the half-dozen steps, and the heels of her shoes clicked loudly on the quarry tiles when she walked the short distance towards the door. Her heart was beating in her throat, and her hand was shaking visibly when she pressed the button beside the door. She could hear the bell chiming somewhere in the house, and moments later the door was opened by a white-coated black man.

'I'd like to see Professor Venniker,' she answered to his polite query, and the door was opened wider to admit her into a spacious, thickly carpeted entrance hall which was bare except for a small rosewood table being used as a telephone stand.

She was led across the hall, past the wide staircase, and down a right turning passage towards a door which stood slightly ajar. The man knocked and stepped into the room. 'A lady to see you, sir.'

Christie could not hear Lyle's reply, she was deaf to everything except the thundering beat of her heart, and then she was being gestured into that room while the black man retreated silently. She swallowed nervously, scraped together her flagging courage, and entered the room, but the next instant everything seemed to freeze inside her.

Sonia Deacon was leaning against the mantelshelf in the book-lined study, and Lyle was standing close to her with a look of annoyance on his face as if he disliked this intrusion. Christie felt as if she had turned into a solid block of ice, and the pain that accompanied it was so intense that she had to clench her jaw for fear of crying out with the agony of it.

'It seems to me, darling, you can forget about that peaceful, quiet evening, you were hoping for,' Sonia purred into the awkward silence, while a slender, scarlet-tipped hand reached out to clasp his arm possessively, and that gesture spoke louder than words. 'He's mine, and don't you forget it!' it said.

'What can I do for you?' Lyle asked, his features granite-hard, and his voice coldly impersonal as if he was addressing a stranger.

Christie stood white-faced and frozen. She tried to speak, but no sound passed her stiff lips, and Lyle's sudden burst of harsh laughter mocked her ruthlessly.

'Are you going to stand there all evening without giving me an explanation for your intrusion into my home?' he demanded bitingly.

Christie felt as if she had become enmeshed in a nightmare from which there was no escape, and somewhere deep down inside her a door slammed shut. 'I—I was hoping that I could—could talk to you about something important, but there—there's no longer the necessity for it.'

Sonia's beautiful features adopted a look of angelic concern. 'If I'm in the way, then I'm perfectly willing to leave you alone for a while.'

'That won't be necessary!' Christie bit out the words.

'Well, if you're sure . . .' Sonia's voice tapered off into a clever and significant silence, but Christie knew that her consideration was as false as her eyelashes.

The only thing Christie wanted at that moment was to get out of that house as fast as her trembling legs would carry her, but she still had some unfinished business to attend to. Her hand dipped into the pocket of her jacket and emerged again clutching the small blue pouch. Her fingers tightened about it jealously for a brief moment, then a smile of self-mockery curved her wide mouth.

'I have something which belongs to you, Lyle.' Her voice was choked with suppressed tears as she dropped the pouch on to his desk, and with it she shed the last fragment of her foolish hopes and dreams. 'Goodbye ... and good luck,' she added in a thin whisper, then she turned and fled.

Christie's running footsteps made no sound on the carpeted floor in the hall, and she was almost blind with pain when she wrenched open the door and raced out into the darkness of the garden. Her fingers were so cold that it seemed to take ages before she succeeded in fumbling the key into her car's ignition, but the next instant she pulled away from the curb with a speed that made the tyres squeal on the tarmac.

He had lied to her about Sonia! That was the only thought stabbing through her tortured mind as she gripped the steering wheel and stared straight ahead of her with dry, stinging eyes. He had lied to her about Sonia, and he had made her believe that there was a chance they could recapture what they had once had. Oh, what a fool she had been! What an idiot!

The traffic lights stopped her at an intersection, and she tapped her fingers impatiently against the steering wheel as a cold, frightening anger took possession of her, shutting out the pain. Lyle would never again have the opportunity to humiliate her like this. *Never again!*

The lights changed to green and she put her foot down hard on the accelerator. The Mazda shot across the white line, and suddenly there was a car bearing down on her from the left. She was aware of its headlights stabbing at her eyes as she tried to avoid it, but her state of mind had slowed down her reflexes, and seconds later she felt a crunching jolt as the car collided with her Mazda.

In her haste to get away from Lyle's house she had neglected to use her safety belt, and the impact flung her forward like a lifeless doll. There was a stabbing pain in her head as it slammed against the steering wheel. Light and sound was magnified for an instant, then a blanket of darkness shifted over her.

Christie could not recall afterwards whether she had regained consciousness slightly, or whether she had simply had a weird, cruel dream that Lyle was there beside her, clasping her hand tightly in his. If her mind had simply conjured up his image, then she had not objected to it. She had drawn strength from his imaginary presence, and she had clung gratefully to that strong hand.

It was at dawn the following morning that Christie regained her consciousness sufficiently to realise that she was in hospital. She could not recall for a moment why she was there, and then she remembered the accident and everything that had occurred before it. She had also had a recurring dream that Lyle was sitting next to her bed. She could still see his white, grim face, but there was no one there now, and neither was there a chair next to the bed. It could only have been her subconscious mind which had conjured up his presence.

'Good morning, Mrs Venniker,' a bright and cheery voice greeted Christie, and she frowned at the white-clad nursing sister approaching her bed.

Mrs Venniker?

'How do you feel this morning?' the woman asked while Christie still fought to absorb and analyse her form of address.

'I ache all over and my head is pounding,' Christie confessed as the sister checked her blood-pressure.

'That's only to be expected, but it will ease off as the day progresses,' the woman assured her brightly, checking the reading on the sphygmomanometer and smiling as she freed Christie's arm.

'I haven't broken anything, have I?' Christie moved her body cautiously and winced.

'You have a small cut beneath the hairline of your forehead, and other than that you have a couple of nasty bruises which may make life a little uncomfortable during the next few days.'

A thermometer was pushed beneath Christie's tongue which prevented her from speaking, and cool fingers gripped her wrist to check her pulse-rate. The sister smiled and nodded with something close to approval, and moved down to the bottom of the bed to make the necessary notes on the chart which hung there conveniently.

'When may I go home?' Christie asked the moment the thermometer was removed from her mouth.

'Oh, not for another day, or so,' the sister said, checking the thermometer reading and recording it on the chart. 'The doctor will want to be absolutely sure that you're in tip-top condition before he allows you to leave here.'

Christie raised a hand to her forehead and her fingers tentatively explored the neat row of stitches. Her head was still pounding savagely, but it was not her head she was thinking about that moment. 'What happened to the people in the other car?'

'There was only one person in the other car, but he was mercifully not injured.' The sister smiled, straightening the sheets. 'Your husband said I was to tell you not to worry about your car, and that he would be taking care of everything.'

'My ... husband?' Christie asked weakly, her eyes following the brisk professionality of the woman's movements.

'He spent the night sitting next to your bed and, if I hadn't insisted that he go home and get some rest, he would still have been here.'

'My *husband*?' Christie asked again, her head pounding worse than before, and her mind whirling with scattered thoughts.

'Yes, dear,' the woman smiled curiously. 'Professor Venniker.'

'Oh, God!' Christie groaned. It had not been a dream, or a hallucination. It *had* been Lyle who had sat so grim and white next to her bed all night. But why? *Why?*

'You're not suffering from amnesia now, are you?' the sister enquired jokingly, but Christie was beyond the stage where she could appreciate it.

Something exploded inside her that brought her close to the point of hysteria, and she snapped at the sister, 'If he comes again I don't want to see him.'

'But he——'

'I don't want to see him!' Her voice was shrill with agitation, and a blinding pain shot through her head when she tried to sit up. 'I tell you I don't want to see him!'

'Now, calm down, my dear,' the Sister instructed, her hands on Christie's shoulders in an attempt to lower her back against the pillows. 'We can't have you upsetting yourself this way.'

'I don't want to see him!' Christie hissed frantically through her teeth while she fought off those restraining hands. She had suffered enough because of Lyle, and she was not going to let him humiliate her once again.

'You shan't see him, if that's what you want, and you have my word on that.' The sister's calm voice finally penetrated through that wall of pain, and Christie slumped weakly against the pillows.

'Oh I wish I was dead!' she croaked, and then she lapsed into a bout of uncontrollable, near-hysterical weeping.

She was behaving like an idiot, but she could not control herself. Her mind was spinning wildly, and painful images flashed cruelly before her eyes. Reality became distorted, and it felt as if she was losing her grip on her sanity, but those images remained with disturbing clarity. Lyle and Sonia were illuminated in the lights of an oncoming car, and they were laughing ... laughing ... and far into the distant past a legendary chieftainess was ... *laughing*! Their laughter went on and on. Or was it her own? A black mamba reared it head and struck. Christie felt its venomous fangs jabbing into her arm, and the mocking laughter began to fade as she drifted off into an ever-narrowing tunnel of darkness.

It was some hours before Christie came to her senses again. Her head felt lighter, and her body felt stiff and bruised, but her mind was still filled with anxiety until the sister assured her that Lyle had been instructed not to come and see her. Only then did a calmness begin to surge through her, and she drifted into a natural sleep from which she did not awake until early evening. A tray of food was brought to her of which she ate a little, and she promptly went to sleep again.

Christie awoke on the morning of her second day in hospital to find the sister with the cheery features hovering over her again. 'Are you feeling better this morning, Mrs Venniker?'

Christie opened her mouth to protest against the *Mrs Venniker*, but, when she thought of the effort it would take to explain, she said simply, 'I'm much better, thank you.'

'You gave me quite a scare yesterday morning, and I'm afraid I had to give you a sedative to calm you,' the woman explained as she went through the same ritual of taking Christie's blood-pressure, pulse-rate and temperature. 'The doctor will be seeing you shortly.'

'I want to go home,' Christie complained almost childishly. 'Do you think he'll let me go?'

'Perhaps,' the sister smiled, 'but my guess is he will want to keep you here another night.'

The sister was right. Despite Christie's insistence that she was well enough to go home, the doctor was adamant that he would not release her until the following day. She could get up and sit in a chair, if she felt strong enough, but she had to spend another twenty-four hours in hospital for observation.

It was futile to argue, Christie could see that, so she spent the day leafing through magazines, and being thoroughly bored with herself. She was in a semi-private ward, but no one occupied the other bed, and she was glad of that. She wanted to be alone, she needed to think, but somehow her mind shied away from everything which veered towards the unpleasant.

She was lying back against the pillows with her eyes closed that evening when a familiar voice asked 'May I come in?'

'Dennis!' Her eyes flew open, and she could not hide her delight at having someone there to help her pass the time. 'Pull up a chair and sit down.'

His green eyes smiled at her teasingly when he produced a single white rose from behind his back. 'I must say that the stitches and the bruise adds a very dramatic touch to your appearance.'

'Does it?' She accepted his gift gracefully and brushed the soft petals against her lips to hide her smile. 'You don't think I look very battered?'

'You look ravishing!'

Her smile deepened and could no longer be hidden behind the rose bud. 'I suspect that all this flattery is intended to cheer me up.'

'Naturally,' he grinned, pulling the chair closer to her bed and sitting down. 'There's a notice board at the entrance to the hospital which instructs all visitors that the patients must be left in a cheery mood after visiting hours.'

'Really?'

'Don't you believe me?'

She laughed at his attempt to adopt an injured look. 'No, I most certainly do not.'

'Wise girl.' His expression sobered a fraction. 'You do look ravishing, though, even in that awful hospital nightgown.'

She absently fingered the unattractive garment she was wearing, and during the ensuing silence her expression became grave. 'How did you know I was in hospital?'

'The professor told me about the accident.' The

chair creaked beneath his weight when he leaned towards her urgently. 'He's been very anxious about you.'

'Has he?' she asked casually, avoiding Dennis's eyes and carefully placing the rose in the glass of water beside her bed.

'Why won't you see him, Christie?' She shied away from the subject. She did not want to discuss it, but Dennis was persistent, and repeated his query. 'Why won't you see him?'

'He lied to me about Sonia.' The words were finally torn from her. 'He told me he had broken off his relationship with her, but she was there the night before last when I went to see him at his home, and I didn't get the impression that she was there without his approval.'

Dennis appeared to consider this for a moment before he said, 'You could have been mistaken, you know.'

'I very much doubt it.' She rejected his suggestion cynically, recalling how Lyle had made it very clear that she was an intruder.

'There might be a totally different reason for Sonia's presence in his home that night,' Dennis insisted, 'and the least you could do is give him the opportunity to explain.'

'Does he feel the need to ease his guilty conscience?' she demanded caustically.

'Give the man a chance, Christie.'

'I'm sorry, Dennis, I can't do that,' she retorted coldly, 'so you might as well report back to Lyle and tell him you have failed in your mission.'

'He doesn't know I'm here.'

There was a horrible little silence while Christie digested this information, and she squirmed inwardly when she realised her blunder.

'That wasn't very nice of me,' she murmured apologetically. 'I couldn't help thinking that he had asked you to come and speak to me on his behalf, but I should have known better.'

'The professor is quite capable of looking after his own interests,' Dennis informed her with a sternness he might have copied from Lyle, then a wry smile softened his features. 'But I did think I might succeed in paving the way for him a little.'

Christie stared at him in silence for several seconds before she could trust herself to speak. 'I hope Lyle realises what a wonderful friend he has in you.'

'I'm your friend, too, Christie.' He leaned forward and kissed her on the cheek. 'Don't forget that.'

A warmth surged into her heart for the first time since that dreadful night she had had the accident and, when she was alone moments later, she felt warm, moist tears hovering on her lashes. She dashed them away angrily. There would be no more tears; not for Lyle Venniker. That familiar coldness shifted about her heart again like an armour against the hurt. For the second time in her life she had made a fool of herself over the same man, but it would not happen again. No man was worth the agony she had suffered.

CHAPTER TEN

It was good to be back in her own environment, but the flat felt empty, and so did Christie. She had been sent home from the hospital that morning in a taxi, and she had found the key to her flat among her personal belongings. Someone, possibly Lyle, had detached it from the holder containing her car keys, and for that, at least, she was grateful. Her body no longer ached, but her bruises felt tender, and the cut against her forehead was throbbing slightly. She rested on her bed most of the afternoon, and tried to read, but she found herself staring blankly at the pages without taking anything in.

Christie was not hungry, but she made herself a cheese omelette and a slice of toast that evening, and forced herself to sit down and eat it. She watched a programme on television for a while, but she found it boring rather than entertaining, and she switched off the set to take a shower instead before going to bed. The warm jet of water seemed to pound the tension out of her muscles, and she felt considerably better when she had washed her hair. The silky softness of her nightdress felt good against her skin after the hospital gown, and her wide-sleeved silk dressing-gown was warm despite its thinness. A small towel took most of the moisture out of her hair, but the electric drier did the rest, and with that it felt as if she had shed the last of the hospital atmosphere.

She wanted to go to bed early, but she doubted

whether she would sleep. The doctor had given her tablets which she could take if it was necessary, and with that consoling thought in mind she brushed her hair until the sheen of fire was in it. Her reflection in the mirror was pale and drawn, and her eyes were shadowed with an inner pain and suffering. She had survived once before, she told her image in the mirror, and she would do so again.

The doorbell chimed, jarring her nerves, and she almost dropped her brush. If this was Sammy, then he could not have chosen a worse time to call on her. She was not in the mood for his persuasive tactics, and she was tired of having to think up a polite refusal every time he approached her with a new contract.

She marched through the lounge and opened the door as far as the safety chain would allow, but the man who stood there was not Sammy. It was Lyle! His shadowed features looked grim and tired, but his jaw was set with a savage determination that made her feel uneasy.

'Open up, Christie, I want to talk to you.'

'Go away!' she almost shouted at him, her heart beating fast with anger and something else which she refused to acknowledge. She slammed the door shut and locked it, but the doorbell rang again with more insistence than before. The sound jarred her sensitive nerves, making her want to scream, and it was self preservation that forced her to unlock the door and wrench it open again. 'Will you please go away!'

'I'll stand here ringing your doorbell all night if I have to,' he threatened her, and one look into those hard, glittering eyes told her that he would do exactly that.

'You're a——' She bit back a nasty word and, defeated, she closed the door and unhooked the chain. The door swung open without her assistance, and Lyle was already inside when she murmured a helpless, 'Come in.'

'We both have some explaining to do, and some of the explanations have been long overdue,' he announced harshly, locking the door and turning to face her with a look in his eyes that made her insides quiver.

'Perhaps you're right,' she agreed, releasing the tight rein on her fury which had been simmering for days. 'I think you can start by explaining why I was admitted to the hospital as *Mrs Venniker*, and why you had the gall to tell them you are my husband?'

'They wouldn't have allowed me to stay with you through the night if I hadn't said that I was your husband,' he explained simply, taking off his jacket and flinging it across the back of a chair as if he intended staying for quite some time.

'Did you think that staying with me would help salve your guilty conscience?' she demanded sarcastically, and Lyle's eyes narrowed to slits of anger in his white face.

'All right, if you want the truth, I did feel guilty since I knew I could have prevented the accident if I hadn't been such a stubborn idiot.' He was breathing hard, and his hands were clenched at his sides as he towered over her. 'You left my house at such a breakneck speed that I followed you in my car, and I was almost directly behind you when the accident occurred. *My God, Christie . . .*' He went several shades paler. 'You could have been *killed!*'

'I wish I had been killed!' she shouted at him as

she turned away to hide her anguish. 'God knows, I wish I had!'

'Don't say that!' His hoarse, unfamiliar voice rebuked her sharply, and he was silent for several seconds before he spoke directly behind her. 'I'd like to explain about Sonia.'

'What is there to explain?' She laughed humourlessly while she put a safer distance between them. 'You lied to me about her, and that doesn't need an explanation.'

'She didn't come to my home that evening at my invitation.' A heavy hand gripped her shoulder, and she had only a fraction of a second to control her features before she was spun round to face him. 'She had been given two tickets to the theatre, and she wanted me to go with her, but I refused her. I offered her a drink, and she was on the point of leaving when you arrived.'

It was such a plausible explanation, and he looked so sincere, but she was still cautious. 'Can I really believe that?'

'If our relationship means anything to you, then you will have to believe it,' he said in a clipped voice, straightening to his full imperious height and looking down at her along his beak-like nose. 'Now it's your turn.'

She felt bewildered and must have looked it too. 'My turn?'

'I want to know about that contract Sammy Peterson took such delight in waving under my nose,' he prodded her memory, and he hooked his thumbs into his belt while he waited for her to speak.

Christie was still too angry and too hurt to want to comply with his wishes. She felt cold inside, and her mind was shut to everything except the fear of more pain, but something deep inside her warned her not to cast aside this very last chance with such negligence.

'I didn't sign it.' She heard the words as if someone else had spoken them for her.

'That isn't a good enough explanation.'

'I didn't sign it because I never had any intention of signing it,' she tried again, sitting down heavily in a chair before her legs gave way beneath her, and she clasped her hands tightly in her lap to prevent them from shaking. 'It was simply one of the many contracts Sammy has pestered me with over the past three years. I read them all not to hurt his feelings, but I always return them unsigned.'

'Why don't you sign them?' he demanded, his piercing glance making her shift uncomfortably in her chair.

'I don't sign them because I have no desire to go back to the life I used to lead,' she explained, wishing he would sit down instead of towering over her in that frightening stance. She was having difficulty in thinking clearly, and he was certainly not making it easier for her. 'I suppose your next question is going to be, where did I find the ivory disc, and why didn't I give it to you before?' She finally found the courage to mention that dreaded subject.

'It was in that small black jar you found.'

Her head shot up and her eyes widened incredulously. 'How did you know?'

'Other than myself, you are the only one who is aware of the history attached to those particular artefacts, and I think you must have known that I was hoping to find the copy of the one you already had in your possession. The jar was the most logical place for it to have been hidden, and my instincts told me that I was right.' He sat down on the arm of the chair close to hers and studied her with a faint smile curving his stern mouth. 'You're also a very bad liar, Christie. You always were, and you always will be.'

'If you knew...' Her hands fluttered helplessly in her lap in her search for the right words. 'Why didn't you say something?'

'I came to the conclusion that you must have had a very important reason for keeping that disc and not telling me about it.' His glance held hers compellingly. 'Are you going to tell me about it now?'

Was she going to tell him? *Could* she tell him? Did she have the nerve to risk everything, including her pride, in the act of laying her soul bare to this man who has caused her so much pain in the past? She shied away from the thought, but something warned her that this was one of those moments in time when complete honesty was the only thing which would suffice.

She could not bear to look at him while she spoke, and she got to her feet to walk jerkily across the room towards the window. She drew the curtains aside and stared blindly down into the well-lit street while she scraped together the remnants of her courage.

'I had this—this crazy idea that—that there would be a certain magic involved in uniting the two discs.'

'And, was there?'

'No,' she shook her head slowly. 'No, there wasn't.'

'What were you hoping for?'

She felt rather than heard him coming up

behind her and, when her insides began to shake, she knew that she had to answer him before her courage failed her completely. 'I was hoping that, when the right opportunity presented itself, I would be able to give you the ivory disc in much the same way as Indlovukazi gave it to her secret lover.'

There was a frightening little silence during which she was almost too afraid to breathe, then the deep timbre of Lyle's voice sent a renewed bout of tremors through her. 'Is that why you came to my house that night?'

'Yes.' She laughed and gestured a little wildly with her hands. 'I told you it was a crazy idea.'

'Christie!' He seemed to growl her name, his hands circling her waist, and his fingers biting gently into her flesh below her bruised ribs. 'Do you love me?'

She had no pride left, but he was obviously not satisfied, and her anger rose like a defensive barrier behind which she could hide. 'Haven't I just said so?' she asked coldly.

'Not in so many words.'

'What do you want from me, Lyle?' She broke free of his clasp and spun round to face him with a blaze of fury in her eyes. 'Are you demanding a sworn statement written in my blood so that you may hang it on your wall at home as the prize joke of the century?'

'Christie,' he groaned, reaching for her, but she darted away from him and that magnetism which still had the power to stir her.

'Go away and leave me alone!'

'No, dammit, I won't leave!' he shouted back at her, and chairs and tables toppled precariously as he ploughed his way across the room towards her.

The look in his dark eyes frightened her, and she turned and fled into her bedroom, but Lyle was behind her before she could slam the door shut. His hands were hard on her body, hurting her tender flesh as he stopped her flight, and his arms were like a vice clamping her against his hard frame. A scream rose in her throat when she looked up into his harsh, angry face, but his mouth clamped down on hers and stifled the sound.

Christie had the curious sensation that her mind and her body were spinning out of control. Instead of resentment and anger, she was caught up on a storm of longing which was so fierce that she locked her arms about Lyle's strong neck, and she clung to him as if he alone could offer her safety. Her body yielded against his as her resistance fled, and the hard pressure of his mouth eased against hers until the sensuality of his kiss sent an exquisite fire racing along her responsive nerves. She was trembling when he finally eased his mouth from hers, and she was clinging to him weakly when she realised that her legs would not take her weight.

'Lyle...' she breathed his name in a choked voice and buried her face against his wide chest. 'I have no pride left and, whether you go or stay, it will make no difference to the way I feel. I love you, and I've never stopped loving you.'

'If I'm expected to believe that you love me, then may I know why you were so adamant about getting a divorce five years ago?'

His cynical query confused and bewildered her,

and he did not attempt to detain her when she took an unsteady pace away from him on trembling legs. 'I can't recall that I was so adamant about ending our marriage, but I do remember that you stormed out of our flat and told me to start divorce proceedings since you wouldn't be coming back.'

He laughed shortly, and the harsh sound grated along tender nerves. 'How conveniently you ignore the fact that I wrote to you, and that you never had the decency to answer my letter personally.'

'Letter?' she asked jerkily, an incredible coldness spreading through her body as she stared up at him blankly. 'What letter?'

'The one I wrote to you a week after I arrived in Italy,' he elaborated harshly and, when she continued to stare at him blankly, his features became distorted with derisive fury. 'Don't pretend that you don't know about it, and don't pretend that you can't recall instructing Sammy Peterson's secretary to send me a curt little note saying that you had no further interest in our marriage and that you would appreciate it if I didn't contest the divorce.'

'I don't know what you're talking about,' she croaked, and the truth spilled out involuntarily when there was no change in his expression. 'I was hoping you would write to me since I had a strong suspicion that you hadn't really meant it when you said that you wanted a divorce, and I waited four months before I was finally convinced that you had meant it.' His derisive smile deepened at her explanation, and she cried out in despair, 'Lyle, you've *got* to *believe* me!'

'I'd like to believe you. God knows, I'd like to

believe you, but after going through five years of sheer hell I feel more inclined to call you a liar.' His eyes, ablaze with fury, raked over her white, quivering face which was raised imploringly to his, and he must have found something there to inject an element of doubt into his convictions. His taut features relaxed slightly, and some of the anger left his eyes as he gestured expressively with his hands, but there was no warmth there. 'All right, let's say you didn't get my letter, but if you didn't get it, then I would like to know who did?'

'I—I don't know,' she gulped confusedly, her mind delving frantically into the past for an explanation, and finding none.

'Tell me exactly what happened after I left for Italy.' Lyle forced her to recount the incidents which had occurred during that dark and painful period in her life.

'I was miserable and terribly unhappy because of what had happened. I didn't want to go on that six-week tour, but I had to, and I hated every moment of it. I came back home expecting to find a letter from you, but there was ... nothing.'

'Who collected your post while you were away, and what happened to it?'

'I asked the caretaker to collect it for me, and to send it on to ...'

'Sammy Peterson's office?' Lyle finished for her when her voice petered out into a frightening silence.

Her mind went wild as her thoughts skidded along an unfamiliar path, and the implication was so distasteful to her that she rejected it at once. 'Sammy would never have done such a thing!'

'I suggest you consider that very carefully before you discard the idea,' Lyle warned darkly. 'Sammy never liked me, and he wasn't very happy when you married me. Afterwards he did almost everything in his power to keep us apart, and you can't deny that, so why wouldn't he intercept my letter to you and have his secretary reply to it as if you had instructed her to do so. It was the easiest thing on earth,' he laughed harshly, 'and with me out of the way there was no possibility of you ever discovering the truth.'

It all made such dreadful sense, but her mind stubbornly refused to accept it. 'It's a monstrous thing to accuse him of! Sammy knew how much I loved you and how much I wanted you to return to me. I wouldn't have been able to cope those first four months if it hadn't been for Sammy's support, and it was he who eventually made the wise suggestion that a clean break would help me adjust to the realisation that you no longer cared.'

Lyle's eyes narrowed speculatively. 'Sammy convinced you that I didn't care and persuaded you to start divorce proceedings?'

'Yes,' she nodded, 'he said it was obvious that you had meant what you had said, and that it was silly of me to want to hold on to . . .'

Her voice trailed off into silence again as memories drifted back which made it impossible to continue ignoring the glaring truth. She had returned from her tour to find that Sammy's faithful secretary had resigned. Sammy had brushed the matter aside, saying that they had had a difference of opinion which had made it impossible for them to continue working together, but from Sammy's assistant Christie had learnt that they had had a frightful row about an unethical letter which Sammy had forced his secretary to write. Christie had not considered it of any significance at the time, but from that moment onwards Sammy had literally pestered Christie to start divorce proceedings. Vulnerable as she had been at that stage, she had finally allowed herself to believe that Lyle had never cared for her, and she had gone ahead with the divorce. Many things were beginning to make frightening sense now, and she sat down heavily on her bed when it felt as if her trembling legs wanted to cave in beneath her.

'Oh, Lyle,' she murmured brokenly, 'I think I'm beginning to understand now why I had that feeling I was being accused by you of something I had no knowledge of, and I'm not surprised that you hated me so much.'

'I never hated you.' The bed sagged beneath his weight when he sat down beside her, and strong fingers tipped her white face up so that she was forced to meet his dark, probing gaze. 'It was a shock seeing you again when I least expected it and, when I thought of the hell you had put me through, all the old fury returned, but none of that altered my feelings for you.'

'I'm sorry.' She swallowed back the choking tears. 'What else can I say, except that I'm so terribly sorry.'

His fingers gently caressed her cheek and traced the outline of her quivering mouth. 'If I had trusted my own judgment I would have known that you could never have viewed my letter with such a total lack of feeling that you would have asked someone else to reply to it in such a callous, dismissing manner.'

'Do you believe now that I never received it?' she asked, her pulse-rate quickening as he leaned towards her.

'I believe you.'

His lips brushed against hers with the lightness of butterfly wings, tantalising and provoking. She drew a ragged breath, parting her lips in eager anticipation, and this time his warm, moist mouth shifted over hers with an intimacy that sent little shivers of sensual pleasure racing through her. It also awakened a hunger in her which she had difficulty in quelling, but there was something she had to know, and she dragged her lips from his to bury her hot face against his shoulder.

'What did you write in that letter?' she asked in a muffled voice, and Lyle began to shake with silent laughter.

'If I still had any doubts, then your curiosity has convinced me entirely.'

'Don't tease,' she pleaded, 'and tell me what you had written in that letter?'

'I wrote all the usual stuff a man writes when he has behaved like an idiot,' he said with a hint of self-mockery in his voice as he pressed his rough cheek against her hair. 'I explained that my disappointment at not being able to take you with me had made me angry, that it had been unfair of me to make you choose between our marriage and your career, and that I didn't want a divorce. I asked you to forgive my disgusting behaviour, and I told you that I would make all the necessary flight arrangements if you would agree to join me in Italy as soon as you were free.'

'Oh, Lyle!' She wrapped her arms about his waist and pressed her body closer to his as a mixture of emotions surged through her. There was a piercingly sweet joy in knowing that he had cared after all, and there was also a fierce anger directed at Sammy for having caused them so much pain. 'What are we going to do?' she whispered, her heart heavy at the thought of how she had been deceived.

'Well, first of all I'm going to give you this.' His arms fell away from her and when she sat up she saw that he was holding an ivory disc between his forefinger and thumb. She felt a little dazed when he pressed it to his lips and dropped it into the palm of her hand and, when her fingers closed about it, he was dangling a small blue pouch almost directly under her nose. 'Now it's your turn.'

Her hand was shaking when she took the pouch from him, and she had difficulty in untying the satin cord. There was a certain magic in this moment, and a tingling excitement cascaded through her when at last she dipped her fingers into the pouch and produced the disc she had found in the small black jar. She pressed it to her lips as he had done and, when she placed it in his hand, she asked shakily, 'Does this mean what I think it means?'

'It means that I love you, and that there could never be anyone else but you,' he said in a voice vibrant with emotion, and tears of happiness glistened in her eyes.

'You've never said that to me before.'

'I have never been much good at voicing my feelings, but I was convinced that you would always know how I felt.' He smiled at her with a new and tender warmth in his glance while he brushed away her tears with the tips of his fingers.

'I was convinced until ...' She shook her head as if to rid herself physically of those unhappy thoughts. 'What happens next?'

'You put these away safely so that they will always be together,' he instructed, his smile deepening as he picked up the pouch she had dropped. They placed the discs into it, and Lyle dropped the pouch on to the bedside cupboard before he turned back to Christie and drew her into his arms. 'All that remains now is for you to agree to marry me as soon as I can arrange it.'

She stared at him in incredulous wonder. 'You want to marry me?'

'They say that marriage the second time around to the same woman is always more successful,' he mocked her, his arms cradling her against him while he lowered her on to the bed and held her prisoner with his body. 'Will you marry me, Christie?'

'Yes ... oh, yes,' she whispered, her hands touching his lean cheeks in an attempt to convince herself that this was not a dream, and a choking sob rose in her throat as she flung her arms about him and buried her tear-wet face against his warm throat. 'Oh, darling, I love you so much.'

They clung to each other a little wildly, and kissed with a hunger which would not be stilled. He shifted his position, taking her with him so that they lay full length on the bed, and she welcomed the fiery touch of his mouth as he trailed exquisite little kisses along her throat and down to where his impatient hands had exposed her breast.

'I want you, Christie, and I'm damned if I'm going to wait until it's legal,' he growled, burying his face in the scented valley between her breasts. 'Will you let me love you?'

'I don't recall that you asked the last time,' she teased, a breathless, husky note in her voice when he parted her dressing-gown and tugged at the confining satin ribbon which would give him freer access to her body.

'I was still suffering from the after-effects of seeing that mamba slithering all over you, and I was angry with myself for still loving you and wanting you. Making love to you was not intended as a punishment, but it ended that way, and I despised myself for it afterwards.'

'Lyle . . .' she groaned his name when his hands slid beneath the silk nightdress. 'That was the past and let's leave it at that. This is another moment in time, and we dare not mar it by lingering too much on the past.'

'A moment in time,' he growled thickly, guiding her hands inside his unbuttoned shirt. 'When you sang that song on our last night in the camp I felt myself cracking wide open, and I had to get away before someone noticed what had happened to me.'

She had never before seen him look so tortured, and she felt his agony as if it were her own. 'Darling . . .'

'I did a lot of soul-searching after that, and I decided that, no matter what you had done before, I wasn't going to let you go out of my life again.'

'Lyle,' she murmured impatiently against his lips, 'make love to me.'

He laughed suddenly, a deep-throated, triumphant laugh that was like music to her ears, and perhaps, in some distant moment in time, there was an echo of that deeply satisfied laughter.

Rebecca had set herself on course for loneliness and despair. It took a plane crash and a struggle to survive in the wilds of the Canadian Northwest Territories to make her change – and to let her fall in love with the only other survivor, handsome Guy McLaren.

Arctic Rose is her story – and you can read it from the 14th February for just £2.25.

The story continues with Rebecca's sister, Tamara, available soon.

The Penny Jordan Collection

Two compelling contemporary romances for today's woman by one of our most popular authors.

Tiger Man
"Adoration has always bored me", he announced. Well that was all right with her. She'd never met a man she adored less. But if it wasn't adoration, what was the feeling he aroused in her?

Falcon's Prey
An ordinary English girl marries into a wealthy Arab family. She knows there will be problems. But can love conquer all?

Available from 14th February 1986. Price £1.95.

Mills & Boon

ROMANCE

Next month's romances from Mills & Boon

Each month, you can choose from a world of variety in romance with Mills & Boon. These are the new titles to look out for next month.

RECKLESS Amanda Carpenter
MAN IN THE PARK Emma Darcy
AN UNBREAKABLE BOND Robyn Donald
ONE IN A MILLION Sandra Field
DIPLOMATIC AFFAIR Claire Harrison
POWER POINT Rowan Kirby
DARK BETRAYAL Patricia Lake
NO LONGER A DREAM Carole Mortimer
A SCARLET WOMAN Margaret Pargeter
A LASTING KIND OF LOVE Catherine Spencer
*****BLUEBELLS ON THE HILL** Barbara McMahon
*****RETURN TO FARAWAY** Valerie Parv

Buy them from your usual paperback stockist, or write to: Mills & Boon Reader Service, P.O. Box 236, Thornton Rd, Croydon, Surrey CR9 3RU, England. Readers in South Africa-write to: Mills & Boon Reader Service of Southern Africa, Private Bag X3010, Randburg, 2125.

*These two titles are available *only* from Mills & Boon Reader Service.

Mills & Boon
the rose of romance

SAY IT WITH ROMANCE

Margaret Rome – Pagan Gold
Emma Darcy – The Impossible Woman
Dana James – Rough Waters
Carole Mortimer – Darkness Into Light

Mother's Day is a special day and our pack makes
a special gift. Four brand new Mills & Boon romances,
attractively packaged for £4.40.
Available from 14th February 1986.

Mills & Boon

Take 4 Exciting Books Absolutely
FREE

Love, romance, intrigue... all are captured for you by Mills & Boon's top-selling authors. By becoming a regular reader of Mills & Boon's Romances you can enjoy 6 superb new titles every month plus a whole range of special benefits: your very own personal membership card, a free monthly newsletter packed with recipes, competitions, exclusive book offers and a monthly guide to the stars, plus extra bargain offers and big cash savings.

**AND an Introductory FREE GIFT for YOU.
Turn over the page for details.**

As a special introduction we will send you four exciting Mills & Boon Romances Free and without obligation when you complete and return this coupon.

At the same time we will reserve a subscription to Mills & Boon Reader Service for you. Every month, you will receive 6 of the very latest novels by leading Romantic Fiction authors, delivered direct to your door. You don't pay extra for delivery — postage and packing is always completely Free. There is no obligation or commitment — you can cancel your subscription at any time.

You have nothing to lose and a whole world of romance to gain.

Just fill in and post the coupon today to MILLS & BOON READER SERVICE, FREEPOST, P.O. BOX 236, CROYDON, SURREY CR9 9EL.

Please Note:- READERS IN SOUTH AFRICA write to
Mills & Boon, Postbag X3010,
Randburg 2125, S. Africa.

FREE BOOKS CERTIFICATE

To: Mills & Boon Reader Service, FREEPOST, P.O. Box 236, Croydon, Surrey CR9 9EL.

Please send me, free and without obligation, four Mills & Boon Romances, and reserve a Reader Service Subscription for me. If I decide to subscribe I shall, from the beginning of the month following my free parcel of books, receive six new books each month for £6.60, post and packing free. If I decide not to subscribe, I shall write to you within 10 days. The free books are mine to keep in any case. I understand that I may cancel my subscription at any time simply by writing to you. I am over 18 years of age.

Please write in BLOCK CAPITALS.

Signature _____

Name _____

Address _____

_____ Post code _____

SEND NO MONEY — TAKE NO RISKS.

Please don't forget to include your Postcode.

Remember, postcodes speed delivery. Offer applies in UK only and is not valid to present subscribers. Mills & Boon reserve the right to exercise discretion in granting membership. If price changes are necessary you will be notified.

Offer expires 31st March 1986.

EP86